MEET BASEBALL'S ALL-TIME HEADLINERS!

THE TEAM that started a baseball dynasty and also broke the color line, making Jackie Robinson the first black player in big league history: the 1947 Brooklyn Dodgers.

THE ALL-AROUND COMPETITORS who ended the Dodgers' domination of the mid-'50s, then whipped the powerful New York Yankees in a great seven-game World Series: the 1957 Milwaukee Braves.

THE ULTIMATE SUPER TEAM and one of the most prolific home-run hitting teams ever with record-breaking players such as Roger Maris, Mickey Mantle, Yogi Berra and Elston Howard: the 1961 New York Yankees.

THE BATTLING BALLCLUB that fought with everybody, including each other, but won three straight World Series and became the first modern team to grow mustaches, starting a trend that continues today: the 1974 Oakland A's.

THE ALL-STAR TEAM OF HITTERS who struck fear in the hearts of opposing pitchers to earn the ominous nickname The Big Red Machine: the 1976 Cincinnati Reds.

Here are the superstar teams, the players and power-packed play-by-play action in the book every baseball fan will want to read . . .

BASEBALL SUPER TEAMS

Books by Bill Gutman

Sports Illustrated/BASEBALL'S RECORD BREAKERS
Sports Illustrated/GREAT MOMENTS IN BASEBALL
Sports Illustrated/GREAT MOMENTS IN PRO FOOTBALL
Sports Illustrated/PRO FOOTBALL'S RECORD BREAKERS
Sports Illustrated/STRANGE AND AMAZING BASEBALL
  STORIES
Sports Illustrated/STRANGE AND AMAZING FOOTBALL
  STORIES
BASEBALL SUPER TEAMS
BASEBALL'S HOT NEW STARS
BO JACKSON: A BIOGRAPHY
FOOTBALL SUPER TEAMS
GREAT SPORTS UPSETS
MICHAEL JORDAN: A BIOGRAPHY
PRO SPORTS CHAMPIONS
STRANGE AND AMAZING WRESTLING STORIES

Available from ARCHWAY Paperbacks

BASEBALL SUPER TEAMS

BILL GUTMAN

AN ARCHWAY PAPERBACK
Published by POCKET BOOKS

New York   London   Toronto   Sydney   Tokyo   Singapore

Cover photos: Johnny Bench by Heinz Kluetmeier; Dwight Gooden by Walter Iooss, Jr.; Rickey Henderson by Chuck Solomon; Reggie Jackson by Fred Kaplan; Mickey Mantle by Richard Meek; all courtesy of *Sports Illustrated*.

AN ARCHWAY PAPERBACK *Original*

An Archway Paperback published by
POCKET BOOKS, a division of Simon & Schuster Inc.
1230 Avenue of the Americas, New York, NY 10020

ISBN: 0-671-74099-7

First Archway Paperback printing March 1992

10 9 8 7 6 5 4 3 2 1

AN ARCHWAY PAPERBACK and colophon are
registered trademarks of Simon & Schuster Inc.

Printed in the U.S.A.

IL 5+

For Cathy

Acknowledgments

The author would like to thank the public relations departments of the Los Angeles Dodgers, Atlanta Braves, New York Yankees, Cincinnati Reds, New York Mets, St. Louis Cardinals and Oakland Athletics for their help in sending both materials and photographs necessary for the preparation and publication of this book.

Contents

Introduction

What makes a baseball team "super"? Is it simply winning a pennant, or does the team have to win the World Series as well? Does a super team have to set records, either individually or as a club? Does a team have to stay at or near the top over a period of a few seasons to be designated as super? There is no one answer. A team can be considered super for any of the above reasons, depending on circumstances.

Baseball Super Teams will examine nine teams from both the National and American leagues. It will cover the period from 1947 to 1990. The game of baseball changed a great deal during this time. For instance, in 1947 there were just eight teams in each league. Every game was played on natural grass. A western road trip meant going as far as St. Louis. Ballplayers could not become free agents and jump teams when their contracts were up. Their salaries were so modest that almost all had to work in the off-season. A World Series check was considered an incredible bonus, and just getting to the fall classic was motivation enough for a player to work hard every day. And perhaps the biggest difference was that in 1947 there was only one black ballplayer in the big leagues.

The teams featured here are considered super for different reasons. The 1947 Brooklyn Dodgers had to overcome the prejudicial adversity caused by having Jackie Robinson in its lineup. The rest of the league was hostile toward the Dodgers for breaking the long-standing color line. In addition, the team had a young and inexperienced pitching staff. Yet it persevered and won.

In 1957 the Milwaukee Braves showed what grit and balance could do. They ended the Dodger dynasty and upset the mighty New York Yankees in the World Series. Hank Aaron, Eddie Mathews, Warren Spahn, and Lou Burdette were just a few of the Braves key players. Four years later no one could stop the Yanks. The 1961 Bronx Bombers were perhaps the most powerful team in baseball history (a record 240 homers) as well as a franchise in the middle of a great five-year run. They also had a record 61 homers cracked by Roger Maris. Super, in every sense of the word.

The 1974 Oakland A's won a third straight World Series and were super because they showed they could win under any kind of adverse conditions. No excuses. When everything was on the line, these A's put strong individual personalities aside and came through as a team. So did the 1976 Cincinnati Reds. Known as the Big Red Machine, Cincy destroyed opponents throughout the 1970s and blasted their way to a pair of World Series triumphs in 1975 and 1976.

In the 1980s the St. Louis Cardinals showed that a team could win with speed and determination, and also by adapting their game to a home park with an artificial playing surface. Manager Whitey Herzog's club helped coin the term *turfball*. The 1986 New York Mets had an abundance of talent, as well as character, which allowed them to be at their best when their backs were to the wall.

A true super team of the late 1980s, the Oakland A's managed to blend a group of high-priced individual stars into a team capable of beating anyone. Three straight pennants from 1988–90 solidified their reputation. They were upset in two World Series, however—the only blemish on an otherwise winning record. And in 1990 The Cincinnati Reds showed that a team can come together and be super for one great year. They even gained momentum up to and through the World Series. Under first-year manager Lou Piniella, the Reds won when they had to. When the postseason rolled around, they caught the feeling that all super teams have—they knew they couldn't lose.

Some of these teams may have been better than others. But each one had an individual blend of talent and personality that worked, in some cases for just one year and in others for more. Each, then, was super in its own unique way.

BASEBALL SUPER TEAMS

1947
BROOKLYN DODGERS

When Branch Rickey, the president and general manager of the Brooklyn Dodgers, signed Jackie Robinson to a professional baseball contract in October 1945, it was certainly a historical event. Even though the contract was for Robinson to play for the Dodgers' top farm club at Montreal, it nevertheless marked the first time a black man had been signed to play professional baseball in the modern era. What's more, Robinson was only a step away from the major leagues.

The wily Rickey actually had more than one reason to sign a black player for the Brooklyn organization. He genuinely felt that black players, long relegated to segregated Negro leagues, should be allowed to play in the majors. It was a long-standing injustice that had to be corrected. However, the far-seeing Rickey also felt that the so-called color line would fall sooner or later. And when it did, there would be a wealth of black talent available. So why not be the first?

Rickey knew it wouldn't be easy for the first black player, so he hand-picked Jackie Robinson. He knew he was choosing not only a great and extremely competitive athlete, but also an intelligent man who would understand the significance of what was later termed Rickey's "Noble Experiment."

The older man grilled Jackie incessantly. He told him what to expect and demonstrated the kind of racial harrassment he would have to face. He called Robinson every racial epithet he knew, prompting Jackie to say, "Mr. Rickey, do you want a ballplayer who's afraid to fight back?"

Rickey responded quickly. "I want a ballplayer with guts enough not to fight back. You've got to do this job with base hits and stolen bases and by fielding ground balls. Nothing else."

Robinson played the 1946 season at Montreal and led the International League in hitting with a .349 mark. He had proved that he was ready for the big leagues. The question was, would Rickey promote him to the Dodgers for the 1947 season?

The Dodgers had been one of the fine National League teams throughout the 1940s. With the fiery Leo Durocher as manager, the Dodgers had won 100 games and a pennant in 1941. A year later the ballclub won 104 times, only to finish two games behind the St. Louis Cardinals. It got a little tougher during the war years, but by 1946 the ballclub was back in second, finishing two games behind the Cards once again.

So the Dodgers had to be considered one of the favorites as the 1947 season approached. However, that was before two major events occurred that could well have changed the fortunes of the team. The first was the suspension of manager Durocher for one year by baseball commissioner A. B. "Happy" Chandler. The reasons for Leo the Lip's suspension were never made clear, and the consensus was that it shouldn't have happened.

The result, however, was that the Dodgers were left without their manager and leader. Two days later the second bombshell was dropped. The team announced that it had purchased the contract of Jackie Robinson from Montreal. Branch Rickey had done it. Jackie would be playing with the Dodgers in 1947, becoming the first black man ever to don a big league uniform. Shortly after that the team named veteran baseball man Burt Shotton as the replacement for Durocher. Shotton hadn't managed since his tenure with Philadelphia and Cincinnati in the late 1920s and early 1930s.

Suddenly a team that was co-favored to win a pennant found itself with a new manager and a controversial player. No one could predict how the Dodgers would react. The team would have to deal with a new manager, with playing beside the first black player in major league history, and with opponents who would probably want to shellac them because of that black player. It wouldn't be easy.

Nor were the 1947 Dodgers the super team of a few years later. They didn't have a lot of power, and the pitching staff was young and inexperienced. What they did have was a nucleus of fine ballplayers. Robinson, who had always been a middle infielder, would have to play first. Because he was such a fine athlete, Jackie took to the new position with little difficulty.

Eddie Stanky was the second baseman. Nicknamed the Brat, Stanky was what Durocher called a scratcher

In 1947, Jackie Robinson not only became the first black man ever to wear a major-league uniform, but was the starting first baseman for the pennant-winning Brooklyn Dodgers. Robby became National League Rookie of the Year and went on from there to forge a Hall of Fame career. (*Courtesy Los Angeles Dodgers, Inc.*)

and a diver, a guy who would do anything to win. Pee Wee Reese was the shortstop. Reese would be the Dodger captain of the great teams of the early 1950s. He was a fine player as well as a natural leader. He was often called the most important Dodger by his teammates during dynasty days.

The third sacker was Spider Jorgensen and the catcher Bruce Edwards, a pair of solid journeymen. Carl Furillo was the centerfielder, a good player who would find a home in right once Duke Snider joined the team. Pete Reiser, the one-time phenom whose career was curtailed by injuries, played the majority of left, while the colorful Dixie Walker, "the People's Cherce," was the rightfielder and probably the team's best hitter. Walker, however, was 36 years old.

With the exception of veteran reliever Hugh Casey, the pitching staff was made up of youngsters and inexperienced hurlers. Righty Ralph Branca would emerge as the ace at age 21. Lefty Joe Hatten was 30, but only in his second big league season. Righty Harry Taylor was a rookie, while lefty Vic Lombardi was just in his third season. This was not the kind of staff that appeared to be geared for a pennant run.

As the season opened, the big news remained Durocher's suspension and Robinson's ascension to the bigs. The Durocher situation soon faded and became old news, but with Robinson it was different. There would be no passive acceptance of him. The majo[r] leagues had been all-white for so long that there w[as] resistance almost everywhere. Robinson was [ha]rassed and ridiculed as perhaps no player befor[e or] since. Opposing pitchers threw at him. Infie[lders] tagged him extra hard. Baserunners looked f[or] chance to run him down or come in spikes high. And the verbal abuse never stopped.

Then there were three very overt incidents. The first came when it was rumored that some of the Dodger players were getting up a petition to get Robinson off the team. Branch Rickey headed that one off, saying that anyone who didn't want to play with Robinson would be dealt elsewhere. Southern-born Dixie Walker did ask out, then reconsidered. After the season ended, Walker was traded to Pittsburgh. By the second half of 1947, however, most of the Dodgers had accepted Jackie as an integral part of the ballclub.

The second incident involved the St. Louis Cardinals, who threatened to strike as a team rather than take the same field with a black man. That idea was quickly stifled by National League president Ford C. Frick. Frick acted very quickly, making a strong public statement that he would suspend any player who struck.

"I do not care if half the league strikes," he said. "Those who do it will encounter quick retribution. All will be suspended and I do not care if it wrecks the National League for five years. This is the United States of America and one citizen has as much right to play as another."

So there was no strike. But it wasn't easy for Frick to police each and every game. It was the Dodger players who had to take matters into their own hands. And that's just what happened when the third major incident occurred.

It happened when the Dodgers traveled to Philadelphia to play the Phillies. Phils manager Ben Chapman led an attack of verbal abuse on Robinson. Robby, who had a history of standing up to any confrontation, had a tough time turning the other cheek that day. At one point he seemed ready to charge the Philadelphia dugout. And that was when his teammates showed their willingness to stand by him.

Second sacker Stanky, who was born in Philadelphia but resided in the still-segregated state of Alabama, hollered into the Phils' dugout, "Hey, Chapman, why don't you get on somebody who can fight back?"

At the same time Kentucky-born Pee Wee Reese walked across the diamond and put an arm around Robinson's shoulder. That seemed to settle things and allow both teams to get back to playing ball. There would continue to be resentment against Robinson and the Dodgers for a number of years, but most of the action would be confined to the playing field. In fact, Cardinals' manager Eddie Dyer paid Robinson the supreme compliment when he said:

"You can't intimidate this man any more than you could a player like Frankie Frisch (a Hall of Fame second sacker with the Giants and Cardinals who played from 1919 to 1937). He's like Frisch, in fact. The madder you get him, the harder he's going to try—and the better [he's going to play]."

Rickey always felt that the abuse Robinson took during his rookie year brought the Dodgers closer together as a team. There was little doubt that the Dodgers were squarely in the pennant race, battling the Cardinals (once again) and the Braves for the lead. On paper, the Cards appeared to have the superior hitting team (with Stan Musial, Enos Slaughter, Whitey Kurowski, Red Schoendienst, et al), while the Braves had some brilliant pitching (featuring left-hander Warren Spahn and righty Johnny Sain). But despite everything, the Dodgers hung tough.

They had even adjusted to the change of managers. Durocher had always been a fiery leader, a skipper who made things happen. He was an intense competitor and habitual bench jockey, not averse to yelling "stick it in his ear" as his pitchers got ready to throw. If there was an argument or a brawl, Leo the Lip was always right in the middle.

Burt Shotton, on the other hand, was a laid-back, let-'em-play manager who made out the lineup card and then calmly watched from his seat at the end of the bench. It was said, however, that Shotton was an excellent handler of pitchers and he nursed his young and inexperienced staff through an arduous season.

By the second half of the campaign it became obvious that this Brooklyn team wasn't about to fold. Robinson was beginning to do his thing—get on base, steal, disrupt the pitcher, take the extra base. Walker and Pete Reiser were on pace for .300 seasons. Robinson, Furillo, and Edwards were also threatening to crack the .300 mark. On the mound, young Branca seemed headed for a 20-win campaign and had emerged as the ace of the staff. Joe Hatten was also putting together an outstanding season, as was the veteran Casey.

It would turn out to be a year of great individual performances in the National League. Ralph Kiner of the Pittsburgh Pirates and Johnny Mize of the New York Giants each hit 51 home runs. Sidearmer Ewell Blackwell of the Reds won 22 games and came within two outs of pitching two consecutive no-hitters. Harry "The Hat" Walker (Dixie's brother) won the batting title with a fine .363 average. Rookie Larry

Jansen of the Giants compiled a 21-5 record, while the crafty Warren Spahn finished with 21 wins and a league best 2.33 earned run average. As a team, the New York Giants set a new major league record by belting 221 home runs.

But when the smoke cleared, it was the Brooklyn Dodgers who defied all the odds and won the National League pennant. The Dodgers wound up with a 94-60 record, topping the Cardinals by five full games and the third-place Braves by eight. They had done it without their manager and with all the hostility created by having baseball's first black player in the lineup.

Under the circumstances, Robinson had a super season. He batted .297 with 12 homers and 48 RBIs. He also led the league with 29 stolen bases and would be named the National League Rookie of the Year. There were some arguments for Larry Jansen or Bobby Thomson of the Giants, but Robby played great ball under extremely adverse circumstances. And his Dodger teammates played great too.

Though no Dodger had more than 12 homers (Robinson and Reese), Dixie Walker hit .306 with 94 RBIs. Furillo drove home 88 and Edwards 80. Both hit .295. Reiser hit .309 in 388 at bats. There was no superstar with the bat, but the Dodgers got the job done. Offensively, they only led the league in stolen bases with 88.

Perhaps it was young Ralph Branca who was closest to having a superstar season. The 21-year-old finished with a 21-12 and a fine, 2.67 earned run average. Hatten was 17-8, while Lombardi and Taylor took 12 and 10 wins respectively. Reliever Casey was 10-4 with 18 saves. This was a Dodger team that

Hall of Famer Pee Wee Reese was one of the best shortshops in baseball for nearly two decades. He was the anchor on the 1947 Dodgers and continued to lead the team during their dynasty years in the 1950s. *(Courtesy Los Angeles Dodgers, Inc.)*

didn't have great numbers, but performed when it had to.

Maybe it was too much to hope for a Cinderella ending. In the World Series the Dodgers had to face the powerful New York Yankees. While not one of the greatest Yankee teams, the Bronx Bombers still had Joe DiMaggio, Phil Rizzuto, Tommy Henrich, Yogi Berra, Charlie Keller, Allie Reynolds, and Joe Page. They were a solid ballclub, winning 19 straight games during July and breezing to the American League flag by 12 games.

Though the Yankees were heavy favorites, the Dodgers battled them right down to the final out. The Series had a couple of "firsts." Robinson, of course, was the first black player in a World Series. In addition, it was the first Series ever to be broadcast on television.

It opened at Yankee Stadium with Ralph Branca taking the hill for the Dodgers against the Yanks' Spec Shea. For four innings Branca was perfect, setting down all 12 Yanks he faced. But in the fifth the Bombers erupted for five runs, erasing a 1–0 Dodger lead and going to a 5–3 victory. When Allie Reynolds defeated Lombardi and the Dodgers, 10–3, in the second game, it looked as if the Bombers would romp. They pounded out 15 hits, including three triples, as Reynolds went the distance, striking out 12.

Back in the friendly confines of Ebbets Field, which had less than half the capacity of cavernous Yankee Stadium, the Dodgers rebounded. They jumped on starter Bobo Newsome and reliever Vic Raschi for six runs in the second, had a 9–4 lead after four, and then hung on for a 9–8 victory. Hugh Casey pitched the final two and two-thirds innings for the win. The Dodgers now trailed by just one game.

Then came the fourth contest, a game that was destined to become a World Series classic. The Yanks started Floyd Bevens, a hard-throwing righthander who was often wild and had a 7-13 record during the regular season. Brooklyn countered with Harry Taylor, who never made it out of the first inning. Fortunately, Hal Gregg came on with seven innings of fine relief.

The Yanks got a run in the first and another in the fourth. Brooklyn came back with a tally in the fifth, capitalizing on Bevens's wildness, and scored on two walks, a sacrifice, and an infield out. It was still a 2–1 game going into the bottom of the ninth, but the Dodgers still didn't have a single base hit off Bevens. Up to that time, there had never been a no-hitter pitched in World Series history, and everyone thought this might be another first.

Carl Furillo opened the Dodger ninth with a walk. After Spider Jorgensen fouled out, Al Gionfriddo ran for Furillo and stole second. Pete Reiser came up as a pinch hitter, and Yankee skipper Bucky Harris ordered him walked intentionally, Bevens's 10th walk of the game. Eddie Miksis went in to run for the gimpy-legged Reiser, and the seldom used Cookie Lavagetto came up to pinch-hit for Eddie Stanky.

On Bevens's second pitch Lavagetto slammed a liner off the right field wall, breaking the spell. Not only did Bevens and the Yanks see the no-hitter go out the window, but both Gionfriddo and Miksis came around to score. Lavagetto's pinch double had driven in the tying and winning runs, enabling the Dodgers to even the Series at two games each.

A Joe DiMaggio homer off Rex Barney in the fifth

inning of Game Five proved the winning margin in a 2–1 Yankee victory. The Bombers now had a 3–2 lead as the Series returned to Yankee Stadium for the sixth game. Vic Lombardi took the mound against Allie Reynolds, but neither was around for long. But by the end of the third inning both ballclubs had scored four runs. The Yanks got another in the fourth, but when the Dodgers erupted for four in the sixth, they took an 8–5 lead.

Then in the bottom of the inning the Yanks rallied. They had two on with two out, and the great DiMaggio was at the plate facing lefty Joe Hatten. DiMag got his pitch and lined a deep shot to left center. Al Gionfriddo, who had just come into the game as a defensive replacement in left, raced at full speed toward the fence in front of the Yankee bullpen. With both baserunners already across home plate and DiMaggio almost to second, Gionfriddo made a brilliant catch just in front of the 415-foot sign at the Yankee bullpen. It probably saved the game as the Dodgers went on to knot the Series again with an 8–6 victory.

So it came down to one final game. Hal Gregg started for the Dodgers against Spec Shea. The Dodgers drew first blood with a two-run outburst in the second, driving Shea from the mound and bringing Bevens into the game. The Yanks got one back in their half of the inning, then took the lead with two more in the fourth. Tommy Henrich drove home the go-ahead run. Yankee manager Harris went to his bullpen ace early, and Joe Page checked the Dodgers to just one hit over the final five innings. The final score was 5–2, making the Yankees champions once more. But the Dodgers had given them a real run for their money.

So the 1947 Dodgers weren't world champions. Nor were they as good as the Dodgers teams of just a few years later. By then Brooklyn would have Duke Snider, Gill Hodges, Roy Campanella, Billy Cox, Don Newcombe, Preacher Roe, and Carl Erskine on the roster. These men would join Reese, Robinson, and Furillo to form the nucleus of one of baseball's greatest teams.

But in another sense the 1947 ballclub was a super team, as well, simply because they won despite incredible adversity and limited talent. They were a team without their regular manager. There was internal strife and hostility in the league because of Robinson's presence. The ace of the pitching staff was a 21-year-old kid who had won only eight big league games coming into the season.

Yet this team prevailed in a tight National League race and took the powerful New York Yankees to seven games before losing the Series. One can't do much better than that.

1957

MILWAUKEE BRAVES

In 1952 the Boston Braves finished seventh in the National League race with a 64-89 record. Fans had stopped coming to old Braves Field. In fact, attendance had dropped from 1,455,439 in the pennant year of 1948 to a paltry 281,000 in 1952. Even the great southpaw Warren Spahn had just a 14-19 record in 1952. The team was in a real funk.

Because of the ballclub losing barrels of money, team owner Lou Perini made a startling announcement in March 1953. He said the franchise would be moving from Boston to Milwaukee for the 1953 season. It would mark the first National League franchise shift in 53 years.

The city of Milwaukee embraced their new team with open arms. They couldn't do enough for the ballplayers, all of whom were instant heroes to the populace. They helped the players find homes and helped the team as a whole going through the turnstyles at Milwaukee County Stadium in record numbers. There were 1,826,397 fans the first year, followed by a record 2,131,388 people in 1954. The club would top the two million mark in attendance for four straight years through 1957. By then the Braves had rewarded their fans by building one of the best ballclubs in the big leagues.

In fact, they gave their new fans some excitement the very first year they played in their new home, finishing second in the National League with a 92-62 record. Though they were 13 games behind the powerful Dodgers, the Braves had a core of fine players upon which to build.

Eddie Mathews, a 21-year-old third baseman in just his second season, won the National League home run title with 47, and he drove home 135 runs. First baseman Joe Adcock blasted 18 and drove home 80. Bill Bruton was a fine young centerfielder, and Del Crandall a very solid catcher. Shortstop Johnny Logan hit .273 with 11 homers and 73 RBIs, good numbers for a middle infielder. The solid Andy Pafko checked in with 17 homers and 72 ribbies while hitting .297.

If the hitting was good, the pitching was even better. Spahn was already acknowledged as a great one. In 1953, the high-kicking southpaw was 23-7 with a league best 2.10 earned run average. He had help from a fidgety right-hander who had once been a Yankee farmhand. Lew Burdette was 15-5 and would come back to haunt the Yanks for trading him. Another righty, Bob Buhl, finished at 13-8 and joined the other two to form a very solid big three.

The team was 89-65 in 1954, good for third place. That year marked the debut of a 20-year-old outfielder named Henry Aaron. Aaron was a .280 hitter with 13 homers and 69 RBIs during his rookie season. He broke an ankle in September, but was already looked upon as a coming star. How big a star, no one really knew.

In 1955 the Braves were second again, then in 1956 the club fell one game short, their 92-62 record putting them right behind the Dodgers, who won it on the last day when Don Newcombe defeated the Pirates for his 27th win of the season. But the Braves were still coming. Aaron won his first batting title with a .328 mark, adding 26 homers. Adcock blasted 38, Mathews 37, and veteran Bobby Thomson had 20. Spahn won his usual 20 games, while Burdette took 19 and Buhl 18. There was little doubt that the Braves would be bona fide contenders in 1957.

The team now had Frank Torre platooning with Adcock at first and the powerful Wes Covington taking over in left. The bench was also strong with the likes of Pafko, Thomson, Felix Mantilla, and Del Rice. The big three on the mound were helped by 6′ 8″ Gene Conley, who backed up Bill Russell with the Boston Celtics during the winter; youngsters Bob Trowbridge and Juan Pizarro; and reliever Don McMahon.

By that time Henry Aaron was known as Hammerin' Hank and was a superstar. Mathews wasn't far behind. So the club seemed to have it all, from superstars to role players. And when they promptly won nine of their first 10 games, they seemed well on their way to that elusive pennant.

Warren Spahn was 36 years old in 1957, but showed no sign of slowing down. Bobby Thomson always said that Spahnie and Lew Burdette kept the club loose when they weren't pitching. On the mound both were all business but different types of pitchers. Spahnie was the fastballer early in his career. His heater had a natural rise to it, and batters hit a lot of fly balls. But they rarely got enough of it to hit it out. As he aged, the lefty was able to change his style with little or no loss of effectiveness. Former star Johnny Sain, who helped pitch the Braves to their last pennant in 1948, always marveled at his former teammate.

"Spahnie was able to change over from being mainly a power pitcher," Sain said. "Not many can do that. He came up with a screwball to help when his fastball began to fade, and after that he added a slider. He's also one of the smartest men ever to play the game, and that was why he was able to pitch no-hit games and even come up with big strikeout performances when he was 40 years old.

"In addition, he was completely thorough. He hit well enough to stay in a close game late, fielded extremely well, could run the bases, and had a superb move to first. And because he lasted so long, he knew he had to constantly change before the batters got to know him too well."

Outfielder Bob Hazle, a rookie in 1957, was amazed by Spahn's command and control.

"Just to play behind him and watch him pitch to Crandall was something," Hazle said. "I have never seen such artistry. He would just hit that mitt time after time, setting hitters up with change-ups and sliders inside, then with two strikes bust that fastball over the middle."

Lew Burdette was the perfect foil for Spahn. When they were back-to-back in the rotation, opposing

Three of the Braves' biggest stars helped the 1957 team win the pennant and World Series. On the left is slugging third baseman Eddie Mathews. In the middle is the classy left-hander Warren Spahn, the winningest southpaw in baseball history. On the right is Hammerin' Hank Aaron, baseball's all-time home-run king and the National League's Most Valuable Player in 1957. (Courtesy Atlanta Braves)

teams would have to adjust to two different kinds of pitchers. Burdette threw a sinker, and hitters usually beat it into the dirt. With all his gyrations on the mound, he was always being accused of throwing an illegal spitter. That just made him more effective.

"No matter how big the game, Lew always acted like Lew," said Hazle. "He just didn't believe you could beat him. You had to show him. Give him the ball and he was as cocky as they come. He'd walk right out to that mound and just dare you to hit him."

While Spahn and Burdette were leaders in the clubhouse and on the mound, there really weren't too many leaders on the field. Aaron and Mathews were both quiet guys who did their jobs without fanfare. Even though Hammerin' Hank was now being talked about as the equal of superstars Mickey Mantle and Willie Mays, he led by example only. The veteran Adcock was also the strong, silent type, while shortstop Logan was more or less a free spirit who was combative but often marched to his own drummer. Catcher Del Crandall was a leader, but he was often preoccupied with his pitchers.

So when the club began slumping in May and then into early June, the lack of a field leader became a concern among Braves' management. On June 15 the club made a trade that would transform them from a good team to a great team. They sent veteran outfielder Bobby Thomson, second baseman Danny O'Connell, and pitcher Ray Crone to the New York Giants in return for second sacker Red Schoendienst.

Thomson, of course, began his career with the Giants and was the hero of the 1951 pennant race when his "Shot Heard Round the World" home run beat the Dodgers in the deciding playoff game. In those days he was an outstanding player. But the Flying Scot broke an ankle after being traded to the Braves in 1954 and was slow to regain his old form. With Covington in left, Thomson became expendable. Both O'Connell and Crone were journeyman players who could help a team but wouldn't be stars.

The key was Schoendienst. The switch-hitting redhead had come up with the Cards in 1945 and had already been an outstanding player for more than a decade. He was a smooth fielder and very solid hitter who had been over the .300 mark in four of the previous five seasons, including a high of .342 in 1953. The 34-year-old veteran was hitting .307 at the time of the trade. But he brought more than his hitting and fielding skills to the Braves.

Schoendienst was the field leader the Braves had lacked, a guy who inspired the others to get it done, a guy who wasn't averse to speaking up when he saw something he didn't like. Even the traded Thomson admitted that the redhead provided the glue that brought the entire Braves team together. He was the missing piece to the puzzle, the one player this already fine team lacked.

"It may sound strange," said centerfielder Bill Bruton, "but one player can really make a difference to a team. Red just took over at second and took charge in the infield. I always felt that getting him was the biggest single factor in our team coming together in 1957."

The team would be tested in other ways. Shortly after the All-Star break, the Braves were playing in Pittsburgh. Felix Mantilla was playing short that day in place of Logan. There was a Texas leaguer popped behind second, and Mantilla began running out as centerfielder Bruton charged in.

"Neither of us knew whether we'd reach it or not, so we didn't call it," recalled Bruton. "That's when we collided."

Both players suffered leg injuries. Bruton's was more serious, a torn knee ligament that would require surgery and knock him out for the season. Suddenly the team lost perhaps its best outfielder and top baserunner. How could the ballclub compensate?

Manager Fred Haney assessed the situation and decided to make what could be a risky move. He asked Henry Aaron to move from right to center, replacing Bruton. The risk was that a new defensive position sometimes affects a player's hitting. But Aaron said he'd give it a try and adjusted to the change without difficulty.

Veteran Andy Pafko moved into a right field platoon with rookie Bob Hazle, who was called up from Wichita after Bruton was hurt. Pafko was a solid player who always did a fine job, but it was the rookie Hazle who began making headlines. He came to the majors with a bat so hot it sizzled. It was as if he could do no wrong at home plate.

"I was hot and hitting everything," Hazle recalled. "I was doing Yogi Berra–type hitting, connecting on pitches a foot over my head if I had to. It didn't matter what they pitched me, and I was enjoying every minute of it."

So were the Braves. As often happens with other super teams, things just fell into place. Schoendienst solidified the infield. Aaron moved to center without a hitch. Hazle was hitting a ton, more than compensating for the loss of Bruton. Spahn, Burdette, and Buhl all continued to pitch well. Righty Buhl was especially effective against the Dodgers and always gave the club a boost when they met their big rivals.

It all added up to a 95-59 finish and the first pennant for the great fans of Milwaukee. The Braves finished eight games ahead of runner-up St. Louis, winning the flag rather easily. The fans responded by setting another new National League attendance mark as 2,215,404 of them passed through the County Stadium turnstiles.

The Braves had won it as a team, but also with a whole slew of outstanding individual performances. Aaron, as expected, led the way. Hammerin' Hank had perhaps his greatest season, hitting .322 and leading the league with 44 homers and 132 RBIs. His efforts would result in his being named the National League's Most Valuable Player.

Mathews again joined Aaron in the power parade, slamming 32 dingers and adding 94 ribbies to go with a .292 average. Young Covington had 21 homers, while Schoendienst did his job to the tune of a .310 average. The rookie Hazle hit a whopping .403 with seven homers and 27 RBIs in just 134 at bats.

On the mound it was the big three again. Wind Warren Spahn up, and he would win 20 games. In 1957 Spahnie finished at 21-11 with a 2.69 ERA. Buhl was 18-7 and Burdette 17-9 for the year. Those three carried the pitching load and could compete with anybody.

Now the Braves had one more hill to climb, and it would be a tough one. They had to face the mighty New York Yankees in the World Series. The Bombers had taken three straight American League pennants and were defending world champions. They had a powerful team featuring Mickey Mantle, Yogi Berra, Hank Bauer, Bill "Moose" Skowron, Gil McDougald, Whitey Ford, Tom Sturdivant, Bob Turley, Bobby Shantz, and Bob Grim. They were talented and deep, down to the last man on the bench. The club was managed by the colorful Casey Stengel, the old professor, who juggled players as well as anyone.

Nearly 70,000 fans were at Yankee Stadium to watch the battle of left-handed aces in Game One of the Series. It was Warren Spahn against Whitey Ford in what was expected to be a pitchers' battle. For the first four innings neither team could break through. But then the Yanks got a run in the fifth and two more in the sixth, driving Spahn from the mound. Only a Wes Covington double and single by Schoendienst in the seventh averted a shutout as Ford went the distance for a 3–1 victory.

At one point in the seventh Hank Aaron was up with two on, a bunting situation, yet Manager Haney had him swing, and Ford struck him out. Asked why he didn't have Aaron sacrifice, Haney barked:

"Listen, I don't bunt, especially away from home and with my best hitter up." The Braves were playing to win.

But with their top pitcher beaten, the Braves turned to their second best, sending Lew Burdette to the mound against the Yanks' Bobby Shantz. Burdette had made just two brief appearances with the Yanks back in 1950 before being sent to the Braves the following year as part of the deal that brought Johnny Sain to the Yanks. He was anxious to pitch against them.

Hank Aaron takes one high for a ball. Aaron's keen batting eye resulted in 755 lifetime home runs along with a slew of other great records. Needless to say, he's a member of baseball's Hall of Fame. *(Courtesy Atlanta Braves)*

After a scoreless first the runs began to come. Both teams scored single runs in the second and third, making it a 2–2 game as the Braves came to bat in the top of the fourth. It was beginning to look as if both starters wouldn't last long. In the case of Bobby Shantz, it turned out to be true.

Adcock and Pafko opened the frame with singles. When Covington looped a hit to left center, Adcock scored, and when Tony Kubek missed Enos Slaughter's throw to third, Pafko also scampered home. That was when Stengel gave Shantz the hook in favor of Art Ditmar. But it was one batter too late. Milwaukee had a 4–2 lead.

That was when Burdette suddenly toughened. Sensing a victory, the sinkerballing righty turned stingy. He blanked the Yankees over the final six innings to coast home with the win that evened the Series at a game apiece. Now the two ballclubs traveled to Milwaukee for the pivotal third game.

It was Bob Buhl and Bob Turley on the hill at the outset, and the Yanks broke this one open in a hurry. They scored three in the first, two in the third, and two more in the fourth to open up a 7–1 lead. From there they romped to an easy, 12–3, victory, which included a pair of home runs by Tony Kubek and one by Mantle. Aaron homered for the Braves in a losing cause.

Game Four was almost a must for the Braves, and it turned out to be perhaps the most exciting of the entire Series. Knuckleballer Tom Sturdivant got the call for the Yanks, while Haney went back to Warren Spahn, hoping his ace could even things up once again. But when the Yanks got a quick run in the first, the nearly 46,000 fans who jammed County Stadium began to worry. Would the Yanks continue their onslaught of the day before?

Spahn, however, settled down, and in the fourth the Braves finally showed some muscle of their own. First it was Henry Aaron doing his thing. With two on, Hammerin' Hank slammed a three-run homer off a Sturdivant knuckler to give his team a 3–1 lead. Moments later it was 4–1 as Frank Torre slammed one into the seats.

Given a lead, Spahn mowed down the Yanks as Burdette had the day before. Going into the ninth, it was still a 4–1 game, and the Braves were three outs away from knotting the Series once more. What happened next must have seemed like a scenerio from a movie. The Yanks had two on with two out. Spahn ran the count to 3–2 on first sacker Elston Howard. Then disaster struck. Howard caught a fastball and drove it into the left field seats for a dramatic, game-tying home run.

The large crowd was almost shocked to silence. How could this happen to the great Warren Spahn? But nothing is certain in baseball. Spahnie just had to grit his teeth and go on. In the top of the tenth, an infield hit by Kubek and a triple by Hank Bauer gave the Yankees a 5–4 lead. Now the Braves were in big trouble. It was Milwaukee who was now three outs from defeat.

Veteran Nippy Jones, batting for Spahn, was the first hitter. Jones appeared to be struck on the foot by a Tommy Byrne pitch, but umpire Augie Donatelli said he didn't see it. Jones then showed Donatelli a smudge of shoe polish on the baseball, and the convinced ump awarded him first base. Stengel argued the call but in vain. Felix Mantilla ran for Jones, and

Johnny Logan then blasted a double off Bob Grim, who had relieved Byrne. Mantilla scored the tying run as the fans screamed with renewed hope.

Now Eddie Mathews was up. The third sacker wasn't having a good series, but this time he got his pitch and slammed a long home run to right field for the dramatic game winner. The Braves and Spahn had won it, 7–5. Once again the Series was tied, and now Burdette would return to the mound to square off against Whitey Ford.

This one was a classic, two craftsmen at the top of their games. Only one run was scored. It came in the Milwaukee sixth and after two were out. Mathews beat out a two-hopper to second baseman Jerry Coleman. After Aaron popped a single to short right, Joe Adcock lined another base hit to right, and Mathews scored the only run of the game.

Burdette was magnificent. He scattered seven hits for his second victory of the Series. Milwaukee now had a 3–2 lead in games, and the clever right-hander had thrown 15 straight scoreless innings against the Yanks. It was back to New York for Game Six as the Braves tried to wrap it up with Bob Buhl. Stengel countered by sending Bullet Bob Turley to the mound for the Yankees.

Again the pitching dominated, and the home run was the order of the day. Turley would throw a four hitter, but he won the game by the skin of his teeth. Berra connected for a two-run shot in the third, but homers by Frank Torre in the fifth and the great Henry Aaron in the seventh tied the game at two all. The game-winner came in the bottom of the seventh when Hank Bauer hit a solo shot off reliever Ernie

Johnson. Turley then closed it out, and it was the Yankees' turn to knot the Series at three games each.

Now there was just one game left. Big Don Larsen, who had pitched a perfect game against the Dodgers in the 1956 Series, got the call for the Yankees. Spahn was scheduled to pitch for the Braves, but the Braves hurler was knocked out of the box by the flu. Manager Haney had no choice but to call on Lew Burdette again. This time the right-hander would be going on just two days' rest.

Another Milwaukee pitcher, Gene Conley, didn't feel Burdette would rattle because he was going on short notice.

"Lew had ice water in his veins," Conley said later. "Nothing bothered him, on or off the mound. He was a real chatterbox when he was out there. He would talk to himself, to the batter, the umpire, and sometimes even to the ball."

Yankee fans watched in disbelief as Burdette began retiring the Bombers. Surely the big New York bats would solve the right-hander's offerings this time, especially since he was pitching with only two days' rest. Larsen matched serves with Burdette for two innings, but in the third the Braves broke the ice. A two-run double by Mathews started the scoring and chased Larsen. Then Aaron welcomed reliever Bobby Shantz with an RBI single. Another single and a groundout brought Aaron home with the fourth run of the inning.

Manager Stengel brought a parade of pitchers to the mound as he tried to get his team back in the game. All the time Lew Burdette continued to roll. When Del Crandall homered off Tommy Byrne in the eighth, making the score 5–0, the ending seemed all but inevitable. Burdette finished the game with another seven-hit shutout, making the Milwaukee Braves world champs.

It had been an incredible Series for the veteran right-hander. Burdette had pitched three complete games and two shutouts. When it ended, he had thrown 24 consecutive scoreless innings, coming closer than anyone to matching the legendary Christy Mathewson's three straight complete game shutouts in the 1905 World Series. The Braves had needed every bit of Burdette's pitching prowess.

As a team, Milwaukee hit just .209 in the fall classic, the lowest average of any winning team up to that time. But the slump didn't affect the great Henry Aaron. Hammerin' Hank hit a whopping .393 with 11 hits, 3 homers, 7 RBIs. Of the other Braves, only Frank Torre (.300) and Red Schoendienst (.278) hit above .227. But as they had done all year, the Milwaukee Braves found a way to win.

The Braves would win another pennant the following year, then lose to the Dodgers in a playoff for the flag in 1959. In the 1958 Series they took a 3–1 lead against the Yanks only to have the Bombers come back to win the final three.

But the Braves had a great run. With Aaron, Spahn, Mathews, and Burdette as a nucleus, they put together a Super Team for the fans of Milwaukee during the first decade of major league baseball in that city. Though the franchise would later move again, this time to Atlanta, memories of the 1957–58 team still abound. An exciting, fun team, the 1957 Braves would be interesting to watch today. They could match up with anybody.

1961
NEW YORK YANKEES

In the 1950s and early 1960s the mere mention of the New York Yankees struck fear in the hearts of other baseball teams. After all, these were the Bronx Bombers, the most dominant team in all of the sport. They were more than a one-, two-, or three-year wonder. This team epitomized the word *dynasty*. The Yanks simply had dominated baseball from the days of Babe Ruth and Lou Gehrig in the 1920s.

The Yankees were in the World Series six times in the decade of the twenties, five times in the thirties, five more times in the forties, then an amazing eight times during the fifties. There were several runs of three straight pennants, a run of four straight from 1936 to 1939 and an incredible five straight pennants and World Series triumphs from 1949 to 1953. Coming into the 1961 season, the Yanks were again defending American League champs, though they had lost to the Pittsburgh Pirates in a wild, seven-game Series the year before.

It was a Series in which the Bombers won three games by scores of 16–3, 10–0, and 12–0. They batted .338 as a team in the seven games, had 55 runs, 91 hits, and 27 extra base hits—all World Series records. Yet they were beaten when Pittsburgh won the close ones—6–4, 3–2, 5–2, and 10–9. The final victory came on a ninth-inning, game-winning home run by Bill Mazeroski.

Although beaten, the Yanks retained their reputation as the Bronx Bombers. They had an incredibly powerful team, as they proved by the hitting records they set in the Series. So at the outset of the 1961 season, the team was favored to win once again, unless they were affected by a sudden and unexpected change.

Shortly after the 1960 World Series ended, the Yanks dismissed their longtime manager, Casey Stengel. Ol' Case was almost an institution in the Bronx. He had piloted the Bombers to 10 pennants in 12 years and at the same time entertained fans young and old with his humor and special brand of storytelling in a language and style the press dubbed "Stengelese." Now he was gone, replaced by Ralph Houk, a no-nonsense former third-string catcher. Houk was known as the Major, a tribute to his war exploits.

"I'll never make the mistake of being 70 years old again," said Casey, with his typical droll humor. Age was given as the reason for his dismissal. But the New York press jumped all over Yankee management for their decision.

"Casey imparted warmth to a cold organization," wrote columnist Arthur Daley, "and gave it an appeal that couldn't be bought for a million dollars. He was priceless."

Fortunately for Ralph Houk, he was taking over a team loaded for bear. The 1927 Yanks, a ballclub led by Ruth, Gehrig, Bob Meusel, Earle Combs, and Tony Lazzeri were dubbed "Murderer's Row" and often called the greatest team of all time. Many compared the 1961 ballclub to that team.

Instead of Ruth and Gehrig, this Yankee club had Mickey Mantle and Roger Maris. Mantle was a switch-hitting superstar, the guy who had taken over for Joe DiMaggio in center field in 1952. The Mick had won the coveted triple crown back in 1956 when he walloped 52 homers, drove in 130 runs, and batted .353. He was coming off a 40-home-run season in 1960. Maris was the right fielder who had come to the Yanks in a trade with Kansas City. He had come into his own in 1960 when he clubbed 39 homers and drove in 112 runs, good enough to win him the league's MVP award.

That wasn't all. The team also had power from the likes of Yogi Berra, Moose Skowron, Elston Howard, and Johnny Blanchard. The infield of Skowron, second baseman Bobby Richardson, shortstop Tony Kubek, and third sacker Clete Boyer was arguably the best in the league. And, as usual, the Yanks had role players to spare.

The pitching was also solid. Lefty Whitey Ford was a superstar at the peak of his career. He had help from Bill Stafford, Ralph Terry, Rollie Sheldon, and Jim Coates. None were in Ford's class, but with the Yankee hitting they could do the job. And if the starters faltered, little lefty Luis "Yo-Yo" Arroyo was ready to come out of the pen and shut down the opposition.

Switch-hitting Mickey Mantle slammed 54 home runs in 1961 and wound up with 536 round-trippers in a great Hall of Fame career. *(New York Yankees photograph, reproduced with permission of the New York Yankees)*

There were several other strong teams in the American League in 1961. Detroit had Al Kaline, Norm Cash, Bill Bruton, and Rocky Colavito, along with a pitching staff that featured Frank Lary and Jim Bunning. The Orioles had Brooks Robinson, Jim Gentile, and big Gus Triandos, as well as a kiddie corps pitching staff of Steve Barber, Chuck Estrada, Jack Fisher, and Milt Pappas. While both these ballclubs had fine seasons, they were no match for the explosion of the Bronx Bombers.

Two things were in evidence shortly after the season began. First, baseballs were flying out of American League parks at an astounding pace. It was a slugger's year, and guys like Harmon Killebrew, Gentile, Colavito, and Cash were all swatting a ton of home runs. They were joined, of course, by Mantle and, a short time later, by Roger Maris. The second thing was the power of the Yankees. It was even more awesome than expected. On top of that, Whitey Ford was off to the best start of his already brilliant career. It was difficult to envision the Yankees being stopped.

What some people might forget was that Maris got off to a terrible start in April. He had hit just a single homer for the month (Mantle already had seven), and his batting average was hovering around the .200 mark. He began confiding to friends and then to the press that he felt the team might trade him.

"The Yankees don't keep outfielders hitting in the low .200s" was the way Maris put it.

In May Maris began finding the range. He ended the month with four homers in three days. At the beginning of June, Mantle had hit 14 homers, Maris 12. But these were two guys expected to hit the long ball, and no one was really excited by their pace. Why should they be? The entire team was hitting. Berra, Skowron, Howard, and Blanchard were all flexing home run muscle.

Manager Houk's biggest problem was finding playing time for all his stars. Berra, Howard, and Blanchard, for instance, were all listed as catchers on the roster, so the new skipper had to be a master juggler to get each one quality at bats. The 36-year-old Berra wound up playing more left field than catching while Howard, the Yanks first black player back in 1955, caught 111 games and played first in nine others. Blanchard, normally a third stringer and a mediocre defensive catcher, went behind the plate 48 times and to the outfield on another 15 occasions. All three hit well all season long.

By June the Yankees began to open up their lead. The only team that seemed capable of seriously pursuing them was the Tigers, who were also putting together an outstanding season. But the Bombers were so good that another pennant was a foregone conclusion. In fact, at month's end the focus seemed to be shifting from the pennant race to an individual race. Before long the entire baseball world, as well as many not normally interested in the game, would all be watching.

Both Mickey Mantle and Roger Maris continued to clout home runs. Maris caught fire in June, slamming 15 of them. Mickey kept pace with nine, and at month's end Maris had a 27–25 advantage. That was when talk about Babe Ruth's record began in earnest. The Babe, of course, had set the single season mark of 60 back in 1927 with the Murderer's Row Yankee team. That year Gehrig finished second with 47, and the third highest total in the league was Yank Tony Lazzeri's 17.

But in 1961 it didn't matter that a lot of home runs were being hit. Mantle and Maris began to capture the imagination of everyone, especially when both sluggers had already passed the 30 mark before the season was half-finished. The press dubbed them the M-Boys or the M & M boys and began counting down to 60. Meanwhile, the rest of the Yanks kept pace, and the team continued to win.

Before long the fans got into the act. They openly began pulling for Mantle, the so-called home-grown Yankee, the superstar successor to Ruth, Gehrig, and DiMaggio. Maris, they felt, was an outsider, a guy who came in a trade and was only in his second season with the club. To really keep the record in the Yankee family, Mantle would have to break it.

There was another difference between the two sluggers. Mantle was a powerful switch-hitter capable of hitting the ball out of any park in the league. He often hit so-called tape-measure shots, long majestic home runs that seemed to travel forever. Maris, on the other hand, had a short, compact swing that was perfectly tailored for the short right field porch at Yankee Stadium. He seemed to have the knack of turning the ball into the lower stands and really had his stroke going for him. But Mantle was more of a classic slugger in the Ruth tradition.

Naturally, much of the pressure fell on Maris. Like Mantle, he was rather shy and withdrawn, not at all comfortable with microphones and notepads shoved in his face. Sometimes he even hid and could be curt and surly with the media. The situation grew worse

Roger Maris topped one of baseball's greatest records when he belted 61 home runs in 1961. The slugging right fielder topped the longtime record held by another Yankee, the legendary Babe Ruth. *(New York Yankees photograph, reproduced with permission of the New York Yankees)*

when Baseball Commissioner Ford Frick said that since Ruth had set his record in a 154-game season, Maris or Mantle would have to break it within the team's first 154 games. Ballclubs played 162 games in 1961, and if either broke the record during those final eight games, an asterisk explaining the situation would go beside the new mark in the record book. That caused more debate and controversy.

"I refused to get involved in that debate," Maris would say, later. "I wasn't even thinking record when it all started. I just wanted to do my best and help the Yankees win another pennant."

That still seemed a foregone conclusion. These Yanks could do it offensively, defensively, and on the hill. One sportswriter, watching the developing situation, put it this way:

"Everyone is watching Maris and Mantle," he said, "and missing the fact that this is a very great baseball team. I emphasize the word *team*. The Yankees have an All-Star caliber player at nearly every position, have the best starting pitcher in baseball, and the game's best reliever. Who could ask for anything more?"

By August the team was on a pace to win more than 100 games and the Maris-Mantle home run race continued to occupy the headlines. Neither slugger showed any signs of slowing down. Mantle was ahead into August, but then Maris slammed four homers in four games to make the two stars even at 45 homers each. Roger stayed hot, and a few days later led it by a 48–45 count. Since both sluggers continued ahead of Ruth's record pace, the setting of a new mark was now a distinct possibility.

"It became difficult for either of us to deny that

the record was on our minds," said Maris. "In fact, it was on everyone's mind. We got no rest from it. The whole thing began to embarrass me. We had a lot of other guys having good years. Why not give them some attention?"

It was a tribute to Manager Houk and the rest of the team that they were able to keep their focus completely on baseball. There also was no apparent jealousy about the two outfielders getting the ink and the media coverage. Ford and Arroyo continued to pitch brilliantly, and Skowron, Howard, Berra, and Blanchard were all in the midst of fine seasons of their own.

By September other records associated with the home runs began to fall. Maris and Mantle became the first teammates ever to hit more than 50 each in the same season. On September 8 Mantle hit number 52, and a day later Maris cracked his 56th. That gave the pair 108 round-trippers as a tandem, breaking the old mark of 107 set by—who else?—Ruth and Gehrig. Soon after that a Bill Skowron homer gave the Yanks their 222nd four-bagger as a team, breaking the old mark of 221 set by the 1947 Giants and tied by the 1956 Reds.

Then in the Yank's 151st game of the year Maris slammed his 58th home run. Mantle seemed stalled at 53. So it would be Maris, the so-called outsider, who had the only shot at the record. The pressure on him was tremendous, so great that the hair began to fall out of his head in chunks. His teammates protected him as best they could, but the reporters and broadcasters continued to seek him out.

Maris's 59th homer came in the 154th game. So if he broke the record the so-called asterisk would go

One of baseball's great characters, catcher Yogi Berra was also a Hall of Fame player who was at his best in the clutch. Late in his career Yogi also played left field to keep his still-tough bat in the lineup. *(New York Yankees photograph, reproduced with permission of the New York Yankees)*

in the books. (The asterisk was officially removed in 1991.) Mantle hit his 54th up in Boston, then fell ill and was forced to sit out the remainder of the season, putting Maris on center stage. Roger came through. He finally belted his 60th against Jack Fisher of the Orioles, then hit his record-breaking 61st in the final game of the season, slamming it into his favorite spot, the lower right field stands, off Tracy Stallard of the Red Sox.

"As soon as I hit it, I knew it was gone, number 61," he said. "It was the only time that the number of the homer ever flashed into my mind as I hit it. Otherwise, I was in a fog. I was all fogged out from a very, very hectic season and an extremely difficult month."

The drama of the home run race over, Yankee fans could reflect on a great season. The team finished with a 109-53 record, falling short by one of the 110 victories of the 1927 Yanks. They won the pennant by eight games over Detroit, a ballclub good enough to win 101 times. As a team, the Yanks had set a new record of 240 home runs, a mark that still stands today.

In addition to the homers, the club led the league in all fielding categories—fewest errors, most double plays, and fielding average. Another reason why they were a true Super Team. And the individual stats were just as eye opening.

Besides leading the league in homers, Maris also led in RBIs with 142 and would win the MVP prize for the second straight year. Mantle drove home 128 runs to go with his 54 homers and batted .317. Catcher Howard led the club with a .348 average, slammed 21 homers, and drove in 77 runs. Skowron had 28 round-trippers and 89 RBIs, while Berra had 22 dingers and 61 ribbies. Blanchard finished with 21 homers and a .305 average in just 243 at bats.

On the mound Whitey Ford put together a Cy Young Award season. The crafty southpaw was 25-4 on the year, leading the league in wins and in innings pitched with 283. Terry finished at 16-3, Stafford 14-9, Sheldon and Coates 11-5 each. It was difficult not to win with those huge bats ready to do their thing. The other hero was reliever Arroyo, who made 65 appearances, had a record of 15-5, saved 29 others, and compiled a 2.19 earned run average. It was hard to see any team challenging the Yanks for the world title.

But the Cincinnati Reds would have a try. The Redlegs, under Fred Hutchinson, were National League champs on the strength of a 93-61 season, as they topped the Dodgers by four and Giants by eight games. Cincy had a solid team, with a pair of superstar outfielders who were as good as any in the game. Frank Robinson was the club's best player, a future Hall of Famer, who batted .323 with 37 homers and 124 RBIs in 1961. Right behind him was Vada Pinson, a .343 hitter with 16 homers and 87 ribbies.

There was more. First sacker Gordy Coleman had 26 round-trippers and 87 RBIs to go with a .287 batting average, while third baseman Gene Freese had identical power numbers and a .277 BA. Even vet Wally Post still managed to go deep 20 times with 57 RBIs in just 282 at bats. Jerry Lynch was a top pinch hitter and part-timer who contributed a .315 average, 13 homers, and 50 ribbies in 181 trips to the plate.

There was even a big three on the hill. Righty Joey Jay was 21-10, while lefty Jim O'Toole finished at

19-9. Bob Purkey wasn't far behind at 16-12, while relievers Jim Brosnan and Bill Henry had 12 wins and 32 saves between them. On paper the Reds seemed like a good test for the Yankees, especially with Mantle available for only spot duty.

It was Ford against O'Toole in the opener at Yankee Stadium. Ford simply continued with the same brilliance he had shown during the regular season. The Reds couldn't touch him. O'Toole pitched a fine game, as well, but the Yanks went to the weapon that had carried them all year—the home run. Solo shots by Howard and Skowron settled the issue as Ford pitched a two-hit gem and the Yanks won, 2–0.

Ralph Terry took the mound in the second game against the Reds' Joey Jay, and suddenly the Yankees didn't look so unbeatable. It was scoreless for three, but in the top of the fourth Gordy Coleman slammed a two-run homer. In the bottom of the inning Yogi Berra duplicated the feat. After that the Reds began chipping away. They got single runs in the fifth and sixth, and a pair of insurance tallies in the eighth. The final was 6–2, and suddenly the Series was tied with the two teams headed to tiny Crosley Field in Cincinnati for the next three games.

Bill Stafford and Bob Purkey were the opposing pitchers in Game Three. Manager Houk may have wanted to give his team a psychological lift, because he also started the ailing Mantle in center field. For six innings, though, the Yanks looked like anything but the Bronx Bombers. The Reds had a 1–0 lead until the top of the seventh, when the Yanks tied it. Cincy then got the go-ahead run in the bottom of the frame. But in the eighth John Blanchard whacked a

Lefthander Whitey Ford was a Yankee mound mainstay throughout the 1950s and into the 1960s. Known as the Chairman of the Board, Ford won 25 games in 1961. *(New York Yankees photograph, reproduced with permission of the New York Yankees)*

pinch homer to tie the game again at 2–2. That set the stage for the ninth.

Purkey was still in the game and facing home run king Maris, who was hitless to that point. But this time Maris connected, sending a long home run deep into the right field stands. The blow would win the game for the Yanks and Luis Arroyo, giving the Bombers a 2–1 lead. Reds Manager Hutchinson always said that Roger's homer was a backbreaker.

"It was definitely the most damaging blow in the Series," said Hutch. "To lose like that . . . we just couldn't seem to bounce back."

The real Bronx Bombers emerged in the next two games. Ford went five more scoreless innings before an injured ankle forced him from the game. But it was enough for the lefty to establish a new World Series record of 32 consecutive scoreless innings. The former mark of 29⅔ belonged to none other than Babe Ruth, when he was a young pitcher with the Red Sox. Jim Coates came on to complete the five-hit shutout as the Yanks took the game, 7–0. Bobby Richardson and Bill Skowron had three hits apiece.

Then in the fifth game it was simply a matter of too many Yankee bats. The Yanks got five first-inning scores to knock Jay from the hill and went on to record a 13–5 victory to wrap up yet another world championship. Blanchard and Hector Lopez homered for the Yanks as they pounded out 15 hits. Lopez had five RBIs, while Skowron drove home three.

Perhaps it was the World Series, even more than the regular season, that fully showed just how super a team the 1961 Yankees were. During the season it was Mickey Mantle and Roger Maris who garnered most of the headlines with their great home run battle. But in the Series Mantle played in just two games and was just 1 for 6. Maris hit the key homer in the third game, but otherwise was just 2 for 19, a .105 average with two RBIs.

But the Bombers still won in five because John Blanchard hit .400 with a pair of homers, Bobby Richardson batted .391 with nine hits, Bill Skowron hit .353, and Hector Lopez checked in at .333 with a team-leading seven RBIs. The Yankee pitchers had a combined, 1.60 earned run average, and Whitey Ford set a new record for consecutive scoreless innings.

So even without their two superstars, the Yankees dominated. That's because the club was talented and deep, explosive offensively and rock solid on defense. This ballclub would win three more pennants during the next three years before the dynasty would suddenly tumble. But the 1961 team will always be remembered. In a sense, they began closing the book, finishing off what the 1927 team had started so many years before.

1974

OAKLAND A's

They came to Oakland in 1968, a team with a reputation for finishing last, a reputation earned at Kansas City, where the A's had gone from their original home in Philadelphia. Now they had made it to the West Coast and, they hoped, a new start. But in the eyes of many, the team already had one strike against it. The A's were owned by Charles O. Finley, a baseball maverick who loved to run against the tide and test the establishment.

Because he didn't have a very good team in Kansas City, Finley was always up to something new, different, and often strange. He once asked his ballplayers to ride the team mascot, a mule named Charley O., before games. Another time he constructed a special "pennant porch," shortening the right field dimensions of his ballpark so that they were identical to Yankee Stadium. Finley claimed the Yanks had an advantage because of their short right field seats and powerful left-handed hitters. The commissioner, however, made him remove the temporary porch almost immediately.

In Oakland it was expected to be more of the same for the team—controversy, Finley's crazy promos, clashes with the commissioner, and more losing seasons. But before the team took the field for the first time in 1968, people began studying the players. The verdict was a surprising one. This was not a bad baseball team.

Charlie Finley had been stockpiling fine young talent, a nucleus of players just beginning to mature. A look at the 1968 team revealed a bevy of future stars. There were young outfielders Rick Monday, Reggie Jackson, and Joe Rudi, a powerful third sacker named Sal Bando, a speedy shortstop in Bert Campaneris, and a slick fielding second sacker in Dick Green. Catcher Dave Duncan was a fine handler of pitchers, and young hurlers Jim "Catfish" Hunter, John "Blue Moon" Odom, and Chuck Dobson were already on board.

There would be no last-place finishes for these A's. They wound up with an 82-80 record for the year and a promise of good things to come. A year later, 1969, marked the first year of division play in the majors. Competing in the American League West, the Oakland A's finished second to the Minnesota Twins with an 88-74 mark. Jackson wound up with 47 homers, Bando with 31. Reliever Rollie Fingers joined the team that year and would become one of the best firemen in the league.

The team also had two different managers in 1969, making it three skippers in two years. Some things with Finley would never change. There was another second place finish in 1970, an 89-73 record, as the team got better and better. Then came 1971, a breakthrough year, under yet another manager, the tough Dick Williams.

That was the year a young left-hander named Vida Blue, in his first full season took the league by storm. Blue finished at 24-8, fanned 301 hitters, had a league best earned run average of 1.82, and was both the Cy Young Award winner and the Most Valuable Player. Catfish Hunter won 21 games, Dobson 15, while Fingers saved 17. The team also hit. Jackson had 32 homers, Bando 24, Monday and first sacker Mike Epstein 18 each, while Duncan slammed 15. All that added up to 101 victories and a first place finish in the West.

Unfortunately the A's had to face a real super team in the playoffs, the Baltimore Orioles, a club that had also won 101 games after winning 109 and 108 the previous two seasons. The Orioles swept the A's three straight games. But that was the last time the Oakland A's would play second fiddle to anyone for three seasons.

In both 1972 and 1973 the A's were simply the best team in baseball, winning the American League pennant, then defeating the Cincinnati Reds and the New York Mets in a pair of seven-game World Series. In the eyes of many, Oakland was a Super Team. If it could win again in 1974, the club would be considered a dynasty.

By then the ballclub already had its identity, and it wasn't always a pretty one. Finley had never stopped being Finley. He broke baseball tradition by putting his club in green and gold home uniforms. He allowed his team to break another long-standing tradition and let them grow mustaches in 1972, bringing back a style from the old days of baseball. For years, players had been clean shaven.

Owner Finley also fought with his managers, who claimed he interfered too much with the day-to-day running of the club. That came to a head in the 1973 World Series when Finley actually fired second baseman Mike Andrews for making two key errors during one game of the Series. The team threatened to revolt, and Baseball Commissioner Bowie Kuhn had to intervene and order Andrews reinstated.

Finley also battled with some of his star players, notably Reggie Jackson and Vida Blue, and the team sometimes battled among themselves, earning them the nickname the Battling A's.

The problems with Jackson began after Reggie hit 47 homers in 1969. Player and owner were far apart in contract negotiations, and Reggie held out. Seven weeks later Reggie signed, but he wasn't happy.

"Sure, I gave in," Reggie said at the time. "But I felt I owed the other guys something. And I still wanted to play baseball, so I signed."

It didn't end there. Finley wanted to teach Reggie a lesson. He ordered him platooned, then benched, and finally threatened to send him to the minors. An angered Jackson asked to be traded. Finley, of course, knew he had a coming superstar and wouldn't consider a trade. But the bitterness lingered. Same thing with Vida Blue. After Blue's sensational 1971 season, he and Finley couldn't agree on a contract. Blue held out. By the time he signed and returned, the season was already underway and he couldn't regain his old form. He went from 24-8 to 6-10.

But in spite of all this, the ballclub won. That was

One of the leaders of the Oakland A's great teams of the early 1970s, Reggie Jackson's clutch performances during playoff and World Series time earned him the nickname "Mr. October." *(Courtesy Oakland Athletics)*

the bottom line. They had character. On the field they always found a way to get the job done. On the field they were together. When Jackson ripped leg muscles in the 1972 playoffs, he couldn't play in the World Series. But he didn't want to leave his teammates and watched the games in civilian clothes from the dugout. Before one game Manager Williams asked Reggie to take the lineup card to home plate, to represent the team.

"It was the only way we could show him just how we all felt about him," the manager said.

But maybe it was Reggie himself who best summed up playing for Charlie Finley during the early 1970s. "There are certain things you have to put up with in Oakland that you wouldn't with other clubs," he said. "But life is too short, and I'm not about to let anything spoil it for me."

Neither were most of the other players. Still, there were more question marks before the 1974 season began. For one thing, Finley had gone through yet another manager. Despite winning two straight World Series, Dick Williams had had enough of Charlie O's interference. The Andrews incident during the 1973 World Series was the final straw. True to his word, Williams resigned, and veteran baseball man Alvin Dark was hired as the new skipper.

The other strange part of this very colorful and successful team was attendance in Oakland. Despite two world championship ballclubs, the fans didn't flock to the Oakland Coliseum. In 1973 attendance topped one million for the first time, but just barely. It was a far cry from the 2.5–3 million attendance today. But even then it was something of a mystery.

"This was clearly the best team in baseball," said

one reporter who covered the team. "They weren't only talented, but they were exciting and colorful. Definitely never dull. Yet the club couldn't seem to catch on with the fans. Maybe baseball just hadn't been in Oakland long enough. But when a great world championship team can only average a little over 12,000 fans per home date, it doesn't make sense."

There was little doubt about the quality of the ball-club. In 1973 Reggie Jackson led the league in homers (32) and RBIs (117) while hitting .293. He would also be the American League's Most Valuable Player. Bando had 29 homers and 98 ribbies, while first sacker Gene Tenace had 24 and 84. Even DH Deron Johnson hit 19 and drove home 81. No wonder they led the league in runs scored.

On the mound Hunter, Blue, and lefty Ken Holtzman were all 20-game winners, while Fingers saved 22 and had a 1.92 ERA. The team was also outstanding defensively, and they could run. Campaneris, who had led the league in steals in 1972, came back with 34 in 1973. New centerfielder Bill North led the club with 53. Both were ready to run again in 1974.

There were also some who said the team was already starting to go downhill, especially when the club didn't look quite as awesome early in the season as it had in the past. In truth, it soon appeared that several of the starters were having off-seasons, especially at the plate. The team batting average was among the lowest in the league.

But because the A's had so many players who knew how to win, they continued to hit in the clutch. And while both Blue and Holtzman weren't pitching quite as well as in previous years, Catfish Hunter was having an absolutely brilliant season. Fortunately, none of the teams chasing the A's was strong enough to make a real run at it. Texas was the only team that had a chance. Spurred on by fiery skipper Billy Martin, the Rangers hung in there but just didn't have enough talent over the long haul.

When the season ended, the A's had won a fourth straight American League Western Division title. They did it with a 90-72 mark, the poorest record for any of the division-winning teams. The reason was mostly because of poor hitting. Tenace batted just .211, second baseman Dick Green .231. Catcher Ray Fosse was mired at .196, while designated hitter–first sacker Deron Johnson slumped all the way to .195. Only left fielder Joe Rudi and shortstop Campaneris were at .290 or above.

Bando led the club with 103 RBIs but hit just .243. Tenace managed 26 homers and 73 RBIs despite his low average, while Jackson clubbed 29 and drove home 93 while hitting .289. Rudi completed a fine all-around season by adding 22 homers and 99 ribbies to his .293 average.

Catfish Hunter had a Cy Young Award season, finishing at 25-12 with a league best 2.49 ERA. Blue was 17-15, Holtzman 19-17. Fingers led the league with 76 appearances and had 18 saves with a 9-5 mark. But because of spotty hitting, there were serious questions about the A's ability to win a third straight World Series.

First there was the business of the playoffs. The A's would be going up against Earl Weaver's Baltimore Orioles, a team that had finished at 91-71 to win the A.L. East. The O's weren't the powerhouse team of a few years earlier. Many of their great stars were aging. But they still had Brooks Robinson, Boog Powell, Paul Blair, Don Baylor, Tommy Davis, Bobby Grich, Mark Belanger, Mike Cuellar, Dave McNally, and Jim Palmer. They appeared to be formidable opponents for the A's.

That theory was quickly advanced in the opener in Oakland when Mike Cuellar bested Catfish Hunter, 6–3, the Orioles scoring four times in the fifth to take a 6–1 lead. Three Baltimore homers by Blair, Robinson, and Grich helped defeat the A's. In a best of five series, losing the opener at home was serious.

What happened next was characteristic of these A's and why they must be considered a Super Team. Though their bats still hadn't come alive (Baltimore's great pitching didn't help, either), the A's suddenly got three brilliant mound performances to sweep the next three games and take their third consecutive American League pennant.

First Ken Holtzman twirled a neat five-hitter as Fosse and Bando homered the A's to a 5–0 victory. Next came Vida Blue. Facing the great Jim Palmer, Blue rode another Bando homer to a 1–0 triumph, giving up just a pair of hits while his teammates managed only four. Hunter and Cuellar returned in Game Four and once again the A's just didn't hit.

But this time the Orioles helped them with their pitchers walking 11 hitters. Oakland got its first run on a bases-loaded walk in the fifth, then Jackson doubled in the second run in the seventh. That would be the A's only hit of the day. Hunter, however, was equal to the task. He threw seven scoreless frames until Fingers took over in the eighth. The Orioles pushed across a run against the big reliever in the ninth but fell one short. The 2–1 victory ended things.

Next the A's had to meet the Los Angeles Dodgers

in the World Series. Winners of 102 games during the regular season, the Dodgers defeated the Pirates in four games to take the National League pennant. Now both clubs got ready for the first all-California Series in baseball history. Dubbed a "freeway" series, many felt the Dodgers had the firepower to dethrone the A's.

L.A. had hitting galore. Steve Garvey led the way with 21 homers and 111 RBIs to go with a .312 average. Jim Wynn belted 32 and drove home 108. Bill Buckner was a .314 hitter while Ron Cey slammed 18 and drove home 97. The catching tandem of Joe Ferguson and Steve Yeager had 28 homers and 98 ribbies between them.

The pitching was also solid. Andy Messersmith was 20-6, while Don Sutton finished at 19-9. Iron-armed reliever Mike Marshall set a major league record with 106 appearances. He had a 15-12 record and 21 saves. He would win the Cy Young Award for his efforts. Secondary pitchers like Doug Rau, Al Downing, and Charlie Hough were also quality hurlers.

Then right before the start of the Series the A's were at it again. First Catfish Hunter claimed that owner Finley owed him back salary and said that unless it was paid immediately, he'd declare himself a free agent based on a broken contract. (Hunter would eventually do this and sign with the Yankees for 1975.) Then Mike Andrews, who was "fired" during the 1973 Series, filed a $2 million libel and slander suit against Finley. And during a workout the day before the Series began, there was a clubhouse brawl between pitchers Rollie Fingers and Blue Moon Odom. But as one writer quipped:

"Now we know things are all right. If the A's

weren't battling someone, I'd worry if they were ready to play."

The Series opened at Dodger Stadium in Los Angeles with Oakland lefty Ken Holtzman opposing righty Andy Messersmith of the Dodgers. Once again the A's were outhit, this time by an 11–6 count. Yet once again they managed to win the ballgame.

They started the scoring in the second. Typically it was Reggie Jackson who did it. Hobbled by a pulled hamstring, the man known as Mr. October blasted a home run into the left center field pavilion to give the A's a 1–0 lead. In the fifth pitcher Holtzman surprised everyone by slamming a double. It was a surprise because the American League now had the designated hitter rule and Holtzman was hitting for just the second time all year. He then went to third on a wild pitch and came home on a suicide squeeze bunt by Campaneris.

A pair of Oakland errors gave the Dodgers a run in the bottom of the fifth. The A's made it 3–1 in the eighth on a Campaneris single, a sacrifice, and a throwing error by Cey. A two-out homer by Wynn in the ninth made it 3–2, and after a Garvey single, Rollie Fingers came on to fan Joe Ferguson, ending the game. The A's were one up.

It was Vida Blue against Don Sutton in the second game. This time the Dodgers jumped on top. They got a run in the second and two more on a Ferguson homer in the sixth. The A's loaded the bases with one out in the eighth. But Bill North then hit into a double play, saved by first baseman Garvey, who scooped a low relay throw out of the dirt in spectacular fashion.

"That was the key play of the game," Sal Bando said later. "If Garvey doesn't catch that ball, we have two runs and a man on second."

But the A's didn't give up without a fight. In the ninth Sutton hit Bando with a pitch, and Jackson doubled to left on a checked swing. Mike Marshall came in the game and Rudi greeted him with a two-run single to left, making it 3–2. The relief ace then picked off pinch runner Herb Washington and fanned Angel Mangual to end the game. The Series was tied at a game apiece.

The victory apparently gave some Dodgers a real shot of confidence, so much so that one was quoted as saying:

"We won 104 games during the season; they won 90. And they look to me like a 90-win club."

A copy of those remarks was pinned up in the A's clubhouse in a place where the players couldn't help but see them. Back at the coliseum, the A's sent Catfish Hunter to the mound against veteran southpaw Al Downing. None of the Dodgers knew it then, but it was the beginning of the end.

The A's drew first blood with a pair of runs in the third inning. The first scored on an error by catcher Ferguson, the second on a Joe Rudi single. In the A's fourth Dick Green walked, was sacrificed to second, and scored on a Campaneris single. Downing was gone, and Oakland had a 3–0 lead.

It stayed that way until the eighth, when Bill Buckner belted a bases-empty homer. Another solo shot by Willie Crawford off Fingers in the ninth made it 3–2, but that was as close as the Dodgers came. The A's had a 2–1 lead as each of the first three games was decided by the same, 3–2, score.

Reliever Rollie Fingers was one of the great closers out of the bullpen in baseball history. You can tell this is an early photograph of Rollie. He doesn't have his trademark handlebar mustache. *(Courtesy Oakland Athletics)*

Game Four was a return match between Ken Holtzman and Andy Messersmith, the opening game hurlers. Once again the A's scored first, only this time it was a surprise. Pitcher Holtzman, who had doubled in the first game, again showed that the designated hitter rule hadn't hurt his batting eye. He slammed a home run over the left field wall to give his team a 1–0 lead.

When the Dodgers got a pair in the fourth on a Bill Russell triple, their fans finally had something to cheer about. But it didn't last long. In the sixth the A's staged a four-run rally without really powdering the ball. But the combination of bloop hits, walks, a wild throw, and force out got the job done, and the result was the same as a grand-slam home run. The outburst made the score 5–2, and that's the way the game ended. Now the A's were a game away from a third straight World Series triumph.

It was Vida Blue against Don Sutton in the fifth game. Once again the Dodgers didn't start well. In the Oakland first Bill North was on first after forcing Campaneris. When he took off for second, catcher Yeager threw the ball into center field, allowing North to move on to third, where he scored on a sacrifice fly by Bando. A Ray Fosse home run in the second made it 2–0 and put the Dodgers in deep trouble.

To the Dodgers' credit, they didn't quit. Though Blue had thrown goose eggs for five innings, L.A. came out scrapping in the sixth. Tom Paciorek, batting for Sutton, lined a double to left center. After Davey Lopes walked, Buckner sacrificed the runners to second and third. Jimmy Wynn then lofted a sacrifice fly to get one run home, and Steve Garvey singled to drive the tying tally home.

Now the Dodgers brought their iron-armed relief ace, Mike Marshall, into the game. Marshall pitched through the sixth, but in the seventh the game took a strange twist. Fans in the left field stands at the Oakland Coliseum began throwing debris onto the field in the direction of Dodger left fielder Buckner. The game had to be held up for some six minutes until the field could be cleared and the fans quieted. Though Marshall threw lightly during the delay, the entire incident might have cost him his edge. The first batter he faced was Joe Rudi, and the A's left fielder went after the first pitch and lined the ball into the left field seats for a home run. That made it a 3–2 game.

Rollie Fingers entered the game for the A's in the eighth, intent on closing it out. The first batter was the aforementioned Buckner, who lined a single to center. When the ball bounced past centerfielder North, Buckner continued on to second. Still not satisfied, he tried to go to third. Right fielder Jackson had come over to field the ball, relayed it to second baseman Green, who whirled and fired a strike to Sal Bando at third. Bando tagged the sliding Buckner on a play that broke the Dodgers' backs.

After that, Fingers closed them out with no further damage, and the A's had done it again. They had won their third consecutive world title! Of the five games four were decided by identical 3–2 scores. And, as usual, when there was a close game, it was the Oakland A's who had found a way to win.

"I don't think anyone can deny the greatness of the A's any longer," said one longtime observer of the team. "These guys have had more problems, on and off the field, than anyone the last three years, and yet they won't quit. They don't care who they are playing. When the chips are down, this team just goes out there with the feeling they will win. All you have to do is look at the results."

It wasn't age or injuries that finally caught up with the Oakland A's of the early seventies. It was the problems with Charlie Finley. Hunter left for the Yankees in 1975, where he promptly won 23 games. Though the team won a fifth straight divisional crown, they were finally beaten in the playoffs by the Red Sox. The next year Jackson was gone, followed by Bando and Rudi in 1977. Vida Blue was gone following the 1978 season.

But from 1972–74 the A's were a sight to see. Colorful and talented, combative and creative, confident and daring, they knew how to win when it counted. And if that doesn't qualify them as a Super Team, nothing does.

1976
CINCINNATI REDS

The Cincinnati Reds of the early and middle 1970s were called the Big Red Machine and with good reason. This was a team that hit and hit and hit, and then it hit some more. The Reds' break-through season was 1970, when they won the National League West with a 102-60 record under Manager Sparky Anderson. The club made it all the way to the World Series that year only to be punched out by the Baltimore Orioles in five games.

They were back in the Series two years later but lost again, this time in a hard-fought seven games against the Oakland A's, a team just beginning a run of three straight championships. But the Reds wouldn't go away. They were N.L. West champs again in 1973, only to be upset in the playoffs by the upstart New York Mets. In 1974 the club won 98 games but finished four behind the 102-60 Los Angeles Dodgers.

So at the outset of 1975, the Reds were a team that still hadn't won a world title. The Big Red Machine always seemed to falter a step away. Some of the problem was pitching. The Reds' arms never really kept pace with their bats.

In 1970, when the team won its first divisional title, the everyday lineup was awesome. Catcher Johnny Bench had an MVP year with 45 homers and 148 RBIs, while hitting .293. Third sacker Tony Perez hit .317, walloped 40 homers, and drove home 129 runs. First baseman Lee May cracked 34 circuits and drove home 94, while outfielder Bobby Tolan checked in at .316 with 16 homers and 80 ribbies. Bernie Carbo hit .310 with 21 homers in a part-time role, while the great Pete Rose was the inspirational leader, hitting .316 with 15 homers and 52 ribbies. The keystone combo of shortstop Dave Concepcion and second baseman Tommy Helms was also outstanding.

Of the pitchers that year young Gary Nolan was the best with an 18-7 record. But Nolan would fall victim to arm miseries and never realize his potential. Jim Merritt, a lefty, won 20 that year but didn't sustain it. Young Wayne Simpson showed potential at 14-3, but fizzled. Only the bullpen excelled, with Wayne Granger recording 35 saves and Clay Carroll 16. Yet despite the thinness in the starting pitching lineup, the 1970 Reds appeared to be a Super Team in the making.

By 1975, however, the jury was still out. The nucleus of the team was still there—Rose, Bench, Perez, Concepcion. The new starters only served to improve the team, once Manager Anderson got a set lineup. Second baseman Joe Morgan had come over in a trade with Houston and was being called by some the best overall player in the game. He could do it all. Left fielder George Foster was a power plant waiting to explode. Outfielder Ken Griffey was a consistent .300 hitter, and centerfielder Cesar Geronimo was an outstanding defender.

Only the starting pitching was questionable. Righty Nolan and lefty Don Gullett both had problems staying healthy. Jack Billingham and Fred Norman, another righty-lefty duo, were good but not great. What the team still had, though, was a great bullpen, now led by Rawley Eastwick and Will McEnaney, and supported by Carroll and Pedro Borbon. Manager Anderson never hesitated to go to his bullpen, and for that he was given the nickname Captain Hook.

Early in the 1975 season the Reds were just not playing great baseball. Manager Anderson had been platooning youngsters Griffey and Foster in right, while the veteran Rose was in left and journeyman John Vukovich played third. Then, suddenly and without warning, Anderson decided to take a gamble.

"An idea just came to me out of the blue," the wily manager admitted. "I decided to ask Pete Rose to move in to third base. Pete had started out as a second baseman, and I felt he could do the job at the hot corner. We needed offense, and John Vukovich just wasn't giving us any. As it was, I had been looking to get Foster's bat into the lineup every day for a year. So I said, why not. I'll try Rose at third if he's willing. That would open up left for Foster and would also give right to Griffey full-time."

The veteran Rose was the key to the move. Would the man they called Charlie Hustle be willing to try yet another position? When Anderson approached Rose, Pete said immediately, "When do you want me to start? Tomorrow?"

Once the changes were made, they seemed like a stroke of genius. Rose took to his new position well, Foster began hitting with renewed power, and Griffey proved another speedy table-setter who could hit .300 and steal a base. It wasn't long before the Reds began to win and win big.

By the second half of the season the ballclub was making a shambles of the National League West race. People were calling them the best team in all of baseball. When it ended, Cincy had won 108 games, third best total in National League history.

The Big Red Machine had simply been overpowering. They scored over 100 runs more than their nearest league rival, were second in doubles, third in homers, made the fewest errors, had the most stolen bases, and the most saves out of the bullpen. It was an overwhelming team performance.

Morgan was the league's Most Valuable Player in a year when the little second sacker hit .327, whacked 17 homers, drove home 94 runs, and swiped 67 bases. He may have been the most outstanding, but he had plenty of help. Bench had 28 homers and 110 RBIs. Perez slammed 20 and drove home 109. Foster hit 23 and drove home 78 in just 463 at bats, hitting an even .300 in the process. Rose batted .317 with 74 ribbies, while Griffey checked in at .305.

The pitchers benefited most from the heavy hitting. Though not one hurler won more than 15 games, nearly every pitcher on the staff was a winner. Nolan, Billingham, and Gullett each won 15, Norman took 12, Pat Darcy won 11, and Clay Kirby was victorious 10 times. Eastwick and McEnaney had 37 saves between them. Only three National League clubs had a

The Big Red Machine of 1976 was a ballclub full of individual stars. But the team's spiritual leader had to be Pete Rose, whose hustle and clutch play set the tone for the entire Redlegs team. *(Courtesy Cincinnati Reds)*

better collective earned run average. So this wasn't a bad group of arms.

From there the Reds made quick work of the Pittsburgh Pirates, taking the playoffs in three straight. Then they had to meet the Boston Red Sox in the World Series. The Bosox had ended the three-year reign of the Oakland A's as American League champs, but the Reds were still the favorites in the Series.

It turned into a great World Series. The two clubs split the first four games, with the last three all decided by one run. The Reds won the fifth game, 6–2, behind Don Gullett, then went for the clincher in Game Six at Fenway Park in Boston. It turned into a classic encounter. The Red Sox took a three-run lead on a Fred Lynn homer in the first, but by the seventh a two-run double by Foster put the Reds out in front, 5–3. Cincy was six outs away from the championship.

By the bottom of the eighth it was 6–3, but then Red Sox Bernie Carbo, a former Cincinnati Red, belted a three-run pinch homer, and the game was tied again. Boston made a bid to win in the ninth, but left fielder Foster threw out Denny Doyle at the plate after a fly ball. In the top of the 11th Morgan looked to hit a go-ahead homer, but Sox right fielder Dwight Evans made a great catch to rob him.

Finally the game went into the bottom of the 12th. Sox catcher Carlton Fisk led off against Pat Darcy and hit a deep drive to left. With a huge national television audience watching, Fisk danced toward first, swinging his arms as if trying to keep the ball from going foul. It was fair, a dramatic game-winning homer, and the Sox had tied the Series again.

The next day the Reds became World Champs. Boston took a 3–0 lead in the third inning, and that was when the Cincinnati Reds finally proved they were a great team. They got two back in the sixth with some nifty baserunning by Rose and a two-run homer by Perez. Then in the seventh they tied it when Griffey walked, stole second, and scored on a Rose single. It was still 3–3 when the Reds came up in the ninth.

Griffey started it with a walk, was sacrificed to second, then went to third on an infield out. After Rose was walked intentionally, MVP Joe Morgan singled to center, and Griffey scampered home with what proved to be the winning run.

Though the Redlegs had finally won it all, they looked to 1976 as another important season. If they could win again, they would move into the realm of a Super Team. As Joe Morgan, the MVP second sacker, put it:

"People say we're cocky because we keep talking about what a good team this is. Maybe that's cocky, but it's not swellheaded. We just know what we can do. We can hit and we can steal and we can go from first to third. Pitching won't stop us. We'll put numbers on the board. All we have to do is go out and play our game, because the best talent is right here in this clubhouse.

"The point is we've all matured together. I think what put this team together was when we lost the pennant to the Dodgers in 1974. That was a low point because we thought we were a lot better team, and since then we've shown it."

Morgan was right. The eight starters on the Cincinnati team going into the 1976 season were all fine players. Morgan himself was being called the most versatile offensive player in the game. Only 5′ 7″, he could generate tremendous bat speed. That's what gave him home-run power. His speed afoot made him a great base stealer, and he had the innate ability to hit in the clutch, witnessed by his World Series–winning hit in 1975.

Johnny Bench was being called the greatest catcher of his generation and one of the best of all time. He was credited as being the first to pioneer the one-handed style of catching, had a great throwing arm, and was an expert handler of pitchers. In fact, when Bench was a 20-year-old rookie back in 1968, he took immediate charge of the Reds' pitching staff. A veteran pitcher on that team was Jim Maloney, who had been one of the best in the National League for several years. Maloney always marveled at how Bench came to the majors and took charge.

"I never thought it would happen," Maloney said then, "but here's this 20-year-old kid actually bawling me out and telling me what to do. He did it all year long. He was like another coach to me. And you know something, I liked it."

Bench could also hit, witnessed by a pair of MVP campaigns in 1970 and 1972. He had clouted 40 or more homers twice coming into 1976 and had driven in more than 100 runs on five occasions. He was a kid that the great Ted Williams once called "a Hall of Famer for sure." Williams was right.

Pete Rose, of course, was a baseball original. Charlie Hustle would become an All-Star at five different positions and wind up as baseball's all-time hit leader. In 1976 Rose was already 35 years old but showed no signs of slowing down. He was a three-time batting champ, a switch-hitter, and a guy who always seemed at or near the top of the league in doubles and hits.

Tony Perez was simply a great RBI man, while Concepcion continued to improve as a shortstop and hitter, his power production increasing almost every year. George Foster was a power hitter of unlimited potential, a guy who would hit 52 home runs in 1977. Griffey was a bona fide .300 hitter who also kept increasing his run production. Cesar Geronimo wasn't a great offensive threat, but he was a fine defensive outfielder who would be a .300 hitter during his best seasons.

The team also had leadership, from Manager Anderson down to Rose, Bench, and Morgan. They had chemistry and the will to win that all great teams have. They demonstrated that by coming out of the gate quickly again in 1976. There was little doubt the Redlegs were serious about winning. As they cruised to another N.L. West title, the Redlegs had their eyes on the Philadelphia Phillies, who were doing the same thing in the East.

Cincy finished the 1976 season with a 102-60 record, six games off the pace of the year before. But offensively, at least, they were more dominating than ever, leading the National League in runs scored (857), doubles (271), triples (63), home runs (141), and batting average (.280). In addition, their 210 steals were tops and their 102 errors the fewest in the league. And once again their bullpen was tops with 45 saves.

Individually, the ballclub was just as imposing. Morgan had a second straight MVP year with a .320 batting average, 27 homers, and 111 RBIs. His power numbers were astounding for a 5' 7", 150-pound second sacker. He also had 60 steals. And he wasn't alone.

While injuries caused Bench to have an off season (.234, 16, 74), George Foster blossomed with a .306 average, 29 homers, and a league best 121 RBIs. Perez was his usual steady self, 19 homers and 91 ribbies, while Griffey had an outstanding year with a .336 average and 74 runs batted in. Rose hit .323 with 10 homers and 63 ribbies, good power numbers for Pete. Dave Concepcion continued to improve as a hitter with a .281 average, 9 homers, and 69 runs driven in. Even Cesar Geronimo batted .307. Good hitting is sometimes catching.

The pitching was a carbon copy of 1975. Nolan was the top winner again with 15 victories. Rookie Pat Zachry won 14, Norman and Billingham 12 each. Don Gullett was 11-3 but again didn't pitch a full season because of injuries. The bullpen of Eastwick, McEnaney, and Borbon had 41 saves, Eastwick getting 26 of them.

While the team had won the division by 20 games the year before, they won it by 10 in 1976. In the playoffs they had to deal with the Phillies, who won 101 during the regular season. The Phils had Mike Schmidt, Greg Luzinski, Gary Maddox, and Bob Boone. They also had a bona fide pitching superstar in lefty Steve Carlton. Philadelphia was a team that wouldn't lie down and die despite going up against the Big Red Machine.

Gullett and Carlton, a pair of southpaws, opened the series in Philadelphia. Though just one game separated the two ballclubs in the regular season, they seemed miles apart in the playoffs. The Phils picked up a run in the first off Gullett, but by the ninth inning it was a 6–1 game, Cincy on top. Foster homered and Rose picked up three hits. A pair of Philly runs in the ninth meant nothing as the Reds prevailed, 6–3.

In Game Two the Phils took a 2–0 lead, only to have the Reds score four in the sixth and two in the seventh to win it, 6–2. Pedro Borbon saved it for Pat Zachry with four scoreless innings of relief. Now it was back to Riverfront Stadium in Cincinnati for the third contest as Jim Kaat went for Philly against Gary Nolan of the Reds.

This was a wild one, the kind of game that again showed the greatness of the Big Red Machine. It was only a 1–0 game after six, the Phils in front. Philly made it 3–0 in the top of the seventh only to have Cincinnati come back with four in the bottom of the inning. But two Phils runs in the eighth and one in the ninth gave them a 6–4 lead going into the final half inning of play.

Once again the Reds showed they had character to prevail. Foster and Bench belted back-to-back homers to tie it, then the Reds pushed across the final tally to win it 7–6 and sweep into the World Series for the second year in a row.

What made it even more interesting was the Reds' opponents. They were the New York Yankees, the Bronx Bombers, returning to the fall classic for the first time since 1964. The Yanks had just come out of their first real sustained down period in more than 50 years. Now they were anxious to prove they could come all the way back to the top.

With the fiery Billy Martin at the helm, the New Yorkers had won 97 games during the regular season, then whipped the Kansas City Royals in five hard-fought games. In fact, they didn't wrap up the American League pennant until the bottom of the ninth inning of the fifth and final game, when Chris Chambliss belted a dramatic home run.

This was not the same kind of Yankee team that had dominated baseball for so long. They didn't have a Babe Ruth, Lou Gehrig, Joe DiMaggio, or Mickey Mantle–type superstar. Catcher Thurman Munson was probably the Yanks' top player. He hit .302, whacked 17 homers, and led the club with 105 RBIs. Munson might have been the best catcher in the American League, but when someone compared him with the Reds' Johnny Bench, Sparky Anderson quickly took up the challenge.

"You shouldn't compare anybody with Bench," said Sparky. "You're just going to embarrass the other human being."

That argument notwithstanding, the Yankees had some other fine players. Third sacker Graig Nettles led the league with 32 homers and drove home 93. Chambliss had 17 dingers with 96 ribbies, while veterans Roy White and Oscar Gamble had 31 homers between them. Speedy Mickey Rivers led the club with a .312 average, drove in 69 runs from his lead-off position, and stole 43 bases.

The Yanks also had some solid starting pitching with Ed Figueroa, Dock Ellis, and former A's star Catfish Hunter. Sparky Lyle was the best relief pitcher in the league. So while the Reds were favorites, there were those who felt the Yankees would give Cincinnati a battle.

Hunter, however, might have sounded a warning. The Catfish had pitched against the Reds in the 1972

Catcher Johnny Bench was one of the National League's top sluggers in the 1970s and, in the eyes of many, the greatest catcher of all time. He is now in the Hall of Fame. *(Courtesy Cincinnati Reds)*

World Series when he was a member of the Oakland A's.

"They're still a good club," Hunter said. "In fact, they might be a little better now."

Manager Anderson called on Don Gullett to open the Series against a surprise choice, Doyle Alexander, a 10-5 pitcher on the year. The first game was played at Riverfront Stadium in Cincinnati, and it was a milestone since it was the first World Series to use the designated hitter, which had been in use in the American League since 1973.

But that didn't bother the Reds. They would set the tone for the game and the Series in the very first inning when Joe Morgan belted an Alexander offering over the right field fence for a home run. It was Morgan who had said that no one could stop the Reds. Now he seemed intent on proving it.

The Yanks managed to tie the game in the second, but then the Reds chipped away. They got another in the third, one more in the sixth, and two final runs in the seventh. Meanwhile, Gullett checked the Yankees on five hits until the eighth inning, when he hurt an ankle by stepping in a hole on the pitching mound and had to leave the game.

Cincy then completed the 5–1 victory to go a game up. The only bad news was the injury to Gullett. It was a dislocation of the ankle that put him out of the Series. At the same time some of the Yankees tried to play down the first-game loss.

"They didn't do anything spectacular out there," said catcher Munson.

Third baseman Nettles added, "We have some pitchers in our league who are better [than Gullett]. Vida Blue throws better, Frank Tanana throws better. But he beat us, so he must be a pretty good pitcher."

Game Two saw Fred Norman start for the Reds against Catfish Hunter, an acknowledged big game pitcher. It was a cold Sunday night in Cincinnati, and Hunter seemed to have trouble getting loose. The A's jumped on him for three second-inning runs. But then Hunter settled down, and his teammates got one back in the fourth and then two in the seventh to tie it. It remained tied at 3–3 as Cincy came up in the last of the ninth.

Hunter was still on the mound, and when he retired the first two Reds, it looked as if the game would go to extra innings. But Yankee shortstop Fred Stanley made a throwing error on a Griffey grounder, and the Cincy right fielder wound up on second. Manager Martin then ordered Hunter to walk Morgan intentionally, but the strategy backfired when Perez rapped a base hit to drive home Griffey with the winning run. Once again the Reds had capitalized on an opponent's mistake.

Leading 2–0, Cincy was confident as the Series went to Yankee Stadium for Game Three. Manager Martin felt his club would now have an advantage.

"We're back home and that gives us an edge," Martin said. "We have our fans, and we don't have their artificial turf."

The Yanks also had Dock Ellis pitching against rookie Pat Zachry. But Ellis lasted less than four innings as Cincy got three in the second and one in the fourth on a Dan Driessen homer, The Yanks fought back to make it 4–2, but two more Cincy runs in the eighth on three singles and a double proved too much for the New Yorkers. The 6–2 final gave the Redlegs a commanding 3–0 lead in the Series. Manager Anderson still felt his team wasn't playing at its peak.

"We have not yet played as well as this club is capable of playing," he said. That was probably the last thing the Yankees wanted to hear.

After a day of rain the two teams returned to action with Gary Nolan opposing Ed Figueroa. Although the Yanks got one in the first even their fans seemed to sense the inevitable. It began in the fourth when the Reds jumped on Figueroa for three runs. Morgan again got it started when he walked, stole second, and scored on a Foster single. A Johnny Bench home run did the rest of the damage.

The Yanks got one back in the fifth to make it 3–2, and it stayed that way into the ninth. Then once again the Reds showed why they were champions. They knew just how to put an opponent away. In the top half of the inning Perez walked and moved to second on a wild pitch. When Driessen walked, the Yanks replaced Figueroa with Dick Tidrow. Two batters later Bench belted his second homer of the game, a three-run shot to left that broke the game open. Doubles by Geronimo and Concepcion brought the fourth run of the inning home, and that was all Cincy needed. McEnaney shut the door in the ninth, and the Reds had swept their way to a second world championship.

It was a dominating performance. The Redlegs hit .313 as a team compared with .222 for the Yanks. They had four homers and 21 RBIs for the four games, while the Yanks managed just one homer and a scant eight runs batted in. Cincinnati pitchers, the team's alleged weak spot, had a Series earned run average of 2.00. Yankee hurlers managed a poor 5.45 ERA. Cincinnati domination was that great.

Now the debate was over. Cincinnati became the first team to sweep both the playoffs and the World Series since divisional play began in 1969. But more important, the Redlegs had shown the world that they were indeed a Super Team. They had taken up where the Okaland A's of 1972–74 left off, exhibiting the same qualities of character, talent, and will to win.

It was the lack of pitching that would short-circuit the team in a bid for three straight the following year as the team faded to second behind the L.A. Dodgers. The club remained a powerhouse hitting team that year, as Foster hit 52 homers and drove in 149 runs. Bench had 31 and 109, Morgan 22 and 78, Driessen 17 and 91. Four of the regulars hit .300 or better.

A great team throughout the early 1970s, a super team in 1975 and 1976, and still an awesome hitting ballclub in 1977, this club had the perfect nickname— the Big Red Machine. They were a steamroller.

1982

ST. LOUIS CARDINALS

The St. Louis Cardinals have one of the great winning traditions in National League history. Since winning their first pennant and World Series in 1926, the Cards have been back to the fall classic on 13 other occasions, emerging victorious another eight times. Most of their title teams had identities all their own, not to mention a wealth of great individual stars.

Among others, the great players helping the Cardinals to win regularly through the late 1960s included Rogers Hornsby, Grover Cleveland Alexander, Dizzy Dean, Pepper Martin, Joe "Ducky" Medwick, Leo Durocher, Frankie Frisch, Rip Collins, Stan "The Man" Musial, Enos Slaughter, Johnny Mize, Mort and Walker Cooper, Whitey Kurowski, Harry "The Cat" Brecheen, Bob Gibson, Lou Brock, Ken Boyer, Steve Carlton, Curt Flood, Orlando Cepeda, Dick Groat, and Tim McCarver. That's quite an array of talent, many of whom are now in the Hall of Fame.

Though the team had some first division years in

the 1970s, they failed to win a pennant or World Series, and their fans were getting hungry. By 1980 the situation didn't seem much better. In the course of a single season the club had four managers and finished with a less than mediocre 74-88 record. There was a handful of fine everyday players, such as first baseman Keith Hernandez, shortstop Garry Templeton, outfielder George Hendrick, and catcher Ted Simmons. But the pitching was weak and the team's future was questionable.

A year later, however, General Manager Whitey Herzog was the full-time field manager as well, and his ballclub surprised everyone by finishing with the best record in the National League East, 59-43. But it was a crazy, strike-shortened split season, and because the Cards were second in each half, they didn't make the playoffs.

Moving into 1982, the Cardinals were something of an enigma. Just what kind of a team was Whitey Herzog gathering around him? Was the split-season record a fluke, or were these guys destined to become winners? Only time would tell, but the ballclub certainly didn't look like the Cardinals teams of the past.

There was almost no power. Only outfielder George Hendrick might qualify as a power hitter, but he was not a 35-40 home run man. No, it was speed that Manager Herzog planned to use to his advantage. The Cards played on artificial turf where speed was a necessity. The wily Herzog felt his ballclub—which emphasized good pitching, defense, the hit-and-run, the sacrifice, the stolen base, and a big man out of the bullpen—could get the job done.

In a sense, it was old-fashioned baseball. And once the Cardinal manager began playing the hand he was dealt, it became obvious that this Cardinal team was in the race to stay. Look at the way the 1982 Cardinals were shaped.

The first baseman was still Keith Hernandez, a former National League batting champ, co-MVP, and a solid .300 hitter. Hernandez was a guy who drove in a lot of runs without hitting too many homers. In addition, he was one of the best fielding first sackers of his or any time. Playing alongside him at second was Tommy Herr, a switch-hitter who could handle the bat and handle the pivot on the double play as well as anyone.

At shortstop was Ozzie Smith, the Wizard of Oz who, like Hernandez, was the top defensive performer at his position in the league. Smith's acrobatic stops and accurate throws brought fans to their feet time and time again. He was also a switch-hitter and a guy who could steal a base. Ken Oberkfell was the third sacker and the weakest link defensively in the infield. But he was a solid contact hitter.

Rookie Willie McGee took over in center. McGee had speed to burn, both in the outfield and on the bases. Plus he gave the Cards their third switch-hitter among the starters, a luxury that few teams have. In left was another newcomer, Lonnie Smith, who came over in a trade with the Phillies. Again it was the same pattern, a player with great speed, only average power, and a base stealer. Hendrick was in right, and Darrell Porter did the bulk of the catching.

The question was pitching. The two top starters were Joaquin Andujar, a fiery right-hander whose temper was often as quick as his fastball, and Bob Forsch, a quiet competitor who rarely seemed to rattle. The two were as a different as day and night, but expected to be big winners. Steve Mura, Dave LaPoint, and young John Stuper were the other starters. Whatever mileage Herzog got from them was considered a plus.

It was in the bullpen where the Cards excelled, and that was almost entirely because of Bruce Sutter. Sutter was a 29-year-old right-hander who had come over to the Cards from the Cubs in 1981 in return for three players. Sutter saved 31 games for the Cubbies in his second year of 1977, and two years later started a string of three straight years in which he led the league in saves, topping it with a record 37 in 1979. Like many great relievers, Sutter had a special pitch. His was the split-fingered fastball, and he was the first to throw that now-popular pitch successfully.

The splitter, as it is called, is gripped wide between the index and middle fingers. A pitcher must have long fingers to throw it successfully, and at that time, not many could. Like many knuckleball pitchers, Sutter said he wasn't sure how his splitter would break.

''I don't try to throw at corners or high and low,'' he said. ''I just try to throw the ball right down the middle.''

Besides his great stuff, Sutter brought a reliever's attitude into the game. Jim Kaat, who was winding down a long and outstanding pitching career in 1982, had been a teammate of Sutter's for just two years. Kaat had both started and relieved since coming to the majors in 1959, and he knew that top relievers had to be cut from a special mold.

''[Bruce] has a special temperament for his job,'' explained Kaat. ''When he goes into a game, it is usually in a crisis. And when he leaves the game, it is either won or lost. But he always has the attitude, 'Give me the ball.' "

Glenn Brummer, the Cards' backup catcher, said that Sutter himself said "that he always thinks he's going to get a batter—somehow, some way. Even if it's a line drive and the left fielder has to make a diving catch for it."

Sutter himself admitted that he had the ability to shake off a bad day and bounce back.

"I know that you'll always have differences one day to the next," he said. "So if I get hit one day, I know it's a good chance it won't happen again. That's what I like about my job. Tomorrow's another day."

Why the emphasis on Bruce Sutter? Simple. With the type of game the Cardinals had to play in 1982, they needed a dominating reliever, a closer, as they say today. They knew there would be a lot of tight games. They weren't going to blow too many teams out, and that big man out of the pen was going to be instrumental in the team's success.

The ballclub started slowly. There were still players getting used to one another and to manager Herzog, who could be tough and demanding. Basically he just wanted his players to listen and then give 100 percent. The way he had his team running, it was as if Whitey Herzog was trying to steal a pennant.

It was the Philadelphia Phils, world champs just two years earlier, who were the Cards' main rivals. The Phils had a superstar pitcher in former Cardinal Steve Carlton, and a pair of aging greats in slugger Mike Schmidt and hustling Pete Rose. They also had a number of other fine players. But they didn't have the secondary pitching and lacked the big closer in the bullpen. If they had Sutter—maybe.

The young Montreal Expos were also an improving ballclub. This team had power with Gary Carter, Tim Wallach, Andre Dawson, and batting and RBI champ Al Oliver. The Expos did have a fine bullpen with Jeff Reardon and Woody Fryman and a fine number-one pitcher in Steve Rogers. On paper, in fact, the Expos might have been the class of the East. And for a while it looked as if they might make it.

It was only after the All-Star break that the Cardinals really took off. Unless you were a fan who lived for the home run, the Cards began showing everyone an incredibly exciting brand of baseball. Hernandez, Herr, and Smith were covering the infield like a blanket. Smith was so good, in fact, that he more than made up for Oberkfell's lack of mobility at third. Herzog was using his ballclub's speed not only on defense, but also on the bases, where the team ran opponents ragged. They forced other teams into errors while their pitchers kept things close. And whenever a game was close, Sutter would usually throw his splitter and close it out.

There were some critics who called the brand of ball the Cards played "turfball."

"They slap the ball down onto the hard artificial turf at Busch Stadium and beat out a lot of infield singles," was the way one writer put it.

Down the homestretch turfball must have been working well. The Cards simply ran opponents into the ground. Both Andujar and Forsch pitched very well late in the season and wound up with a team high 15 victories each. They got surprising (9-3) help from LaPoint and from rookie Stuper (9-7). The rest came mostly from Sutter, who had a 9-8 record, but also saved 36 games. And when the top fireman tired, veteran Doug Bair filled in to the tune of eight saves of his own.

When it ended, the Cards had won the East with a 92-70 record, three games better than Philadelphia and six ahead of Montreal. And they did it by hitting just 67 home runs, lowest total in the major leagues. Hendrick led the club with 19 (and 104 RBIs), but the only other player with double dingers was catcher Porter with 12.

That didn't matter. Hernandez had a typical year at the plate, hitting .299 and squeezing 94 RBIs out of just seven homers. Lonnie Smith was a .307 hitter, hit eight homers, and drove home 69 runs while finishing second to Montreal's Tim Raines in steals with 68. In fact, as a club, the Cards led the league with 200 stolen sacks. Willie McGee had a fine rookie year, batting .296 and stealing 24 bases.

Shortstop Smith hit just .248 but often delivered in the clutch and swiped 25 bases in 30 tries.

"It sometimes annoys me," he said, "because everybody talks about my fielding, but I'm also real proud of my hitting. I think I helped this club offensively."

He did. But his fielding was something to behold. He was often compared to Phil Rizzuto, Pee Wee Reese, Luis Aparicio, and Marty Marion. A former major league player and manager and currently a broadcaster, Jerry Coleman said, "I've been around a long time, and I've never seen a better [shortstop]."

So despite the lack of power, this club had something special. Maybe they didn't look like a championship baseball team, but Manager Herzog had mixed

First sacker Keith Hernandez could have made a big-league career with his fielding ability alone. But the southpaw swinger was also a fine hitter and clutch RBI guy. He helped the Cards become champs in '82 and did the same thing for the New York Mets four years later. *(Courtesy St. Louis Cardinals)*

his caldron of talent well and come up with a formula that worked.

In the playoffs the Cards would have to face the resurgent Atlanta Braves, a team that had started the season with a National League record 13 straight victories. The Braves didn't lose their first game until April 22. But take away those 13 at the beginning of the season, and the Braves were just 76-73 the rest of the way. Add the 13 and they were 89-73, good enough to beat the Dodgers by one game and the Giants by two.

The Braves had the league's Most Valuable Player in Dale Murphy, who clobbered 36 homers and tied Montreal's Al Oliver for the RBI lead with 109. Bob Horner had 32 homers and 97 ribbies, while vets Chris Chambliss and Claudell Washington drove home 86 and 80 runs respectively. These guys could hit.

Ageless knuckleballer Phil Niekro was an amazing 17-4 at age 43, while Gene Garber came out of the bullpen to save 30 games. Big Steve Bedrosian saved 11. Those three formed the heart of the pitching staff. There were some who thought that would be enough to beat the punchless Cards, especially if the Braves could get a dose of the long ball.

Lady Luck smiled on the Cards when the first game in St. Louis was rained out in the fifth inning just a couple of outs away from being official. The Braves had a 1–0 lead with Niekro out in front of Andujar. So the two teams had to start over the next day, and now the Braves were forced to go with young Pascual Perez, who had been just 4-4 as a spot starter. St. Louis countered with Bob Forsch, and it was his day. Perez pitched into the sixth when the Cards erupted for five runs, giving them a six-run lead. That was more than enough for Forsch, who was on his way to twirling a three-hit shutout. The final was 7–0, and the Cards were off and running.

Now Manager Herzog had the luxury of throwing rookie John Stuper in the second game, while the Braves were forced to come back with Niekro, who had pitched in the rainout. Despite obvious fatigue, Niekro had the knuckler working and pitched his heart out for six innings. When he departed, the Braves had a 3–2 lead.

But the Cards tied the game against Gene Garber in the eighth. They did it in typical St. Louis fashion, scoring on a walk, a single, and an infield out. With Sutter throwing the eighth and ninth for the Cards, it was still a 3–3 game as St. Louis came in the bottom of the inning. Rookie David Green pinch-hit a single and was promptly sacrificed to second by Herr. Garber was ordered to pitch to Ken Oberkfell, who lined the ball over the head of Brett Butler in center, and the Cards had won it, 4–3.

The next day the teams were in Atlanta, where Joaquin Andujar with help from Sutter pitched the Cardinals to the National League pennant. St. Louis won the game, 6–2, aided by a four-run second inning. The big hit was Willie McGee's triple, and the rookie added a homer in the ninth as part of the 12-hit attack. Sutter retired all seven batters he faced, and the Cards were headed to the World Series for the first time since 1968.

It would be a World Series of opposites. The Cards would be meeting the Milwaukee Brewers, a team making it to the fall classic for the first time. The Brewers had struggled early in the year, only 23–24 under Buck Rodgers. But when Rodgers was replaced by former batting champ Harvey Kuenn, the Brewers caught fire. They were 72-43 the rest of the way to finish at 95-67, edging the Baltimore Orioles by a single game to win the American League East crown. A dramatic comeback in the playoffs brought the Brewers back from a 2–0 deficit to defeat the California Angels for the A.L. flag in five games.

Unlike the Cards, the Brewers were a slugging team. Nicknamed "Harvey's Wallbangers," the Brew crew belted 216 round-trippers during the year while scoring a league high 891 runs. The ballclub was loaded with lumber. They had five players with 20 or more homers, four men who drove in more than 100 runs, a trio of .300 hitters, and role players who could also swing the bat.

The top hitters were Robin Yount, Cecil Cooper, Paul Molitor, Ben Oglivie, Ted Simmons, and Gorman Thomas, who led the American League with 39 round-trippers. Mike Caldwell and Pete Vuckovich were the top starters, though many considered late-season aquisition Don Sutton (4-1 with the Brewers, 17-9 overall), the team's best money pitcher. Rollie Fingers was the top reliever with 29 saves but would miss the Series with an arm injury. He was one reliever who might have been able to match Sutter.

So as the Series opened in St. Louis, the big question was could the Cardinal pitchers keep the Milwaukee hitters from belting the ball out of the lot? And could the Milwaukee defense contain the speedy, slithery Cardinals on the base paths? Right-hander Bob Forsch was Manager Herzog's choice in the opener, while the Brewers countered with southpaw Mike Caldwell.

Within minutes of the first pitch the 53,723 fans at Busch Stadium must have thought they were in some kind of baseball Twilight Zone. With a couple of Brewers on in the very first inning, Ben Oglivie hit a grounder to Hernandez at first. The best first baseman in baseball bent down to field it—and it went under his glove! So the Series began with the Brewers scoring two unearned runs, and that opened the floodgates.

When it ended, Harvey's Wallbangers had banged out 17 hits and routed the Cardinals, 10–0. Paul Molitor became the first player in Series history to get five hits in a game, while Robin Yount had four. Ted Simmons had the only homer as the Brewers finished it off by getting their final four runs in the ninth. By contrast, St. Louis managed just three scattered hits off Caldwell in a game that left everyone shell-shocked. Maybe the Brewer bats were too much for the Cards after all.

Young John Stuper was on the mound for the Cards in Game Two, facing the veteran Don Sutton. For three innings it looked like more of the same. Stuper didn't have good control, and the Brewers jumped on him for a run in the second and two more in the third. At that point the Brewers had already outhit the Cardinals 22–3 and had outscored them, 13–0. The fans at St. Louis began booing their heroes.

But in the bottom of the third the balance began to shift. With two outs Tommy Herr and Ken Oberkfell both slapped run-scoring singles to bring the Cards within one at 3–2. It stayed that way until the fifth, when Ted Simmons cracked his second home run in as many days to make it a 4–2 game. That finished it for Stuper as veteran Jim Kaat came in to get the side out.

To their credit, the Cards didn't quit. They got a couple of runners on in the sixth with two out, catcher Darrell Porter up. The Milwaukee defense was shifted around to right on the lefty-swinging back-stop, but Porter promptly crossed them up and slammed a two-run double down the left field line to drive in the tying runs.

"That's the first ball I've hit down the third base line in three years," Porter said later. "The shift was right. I just beat it."

With the game tied, the Brewers made some noise in the seventh. They had the go-ahead run at second with two out, and Manager Herzog knew immediately what had to be done. It was time for Bruce Sutter to enter the game. Sutter walked Simmons intentionally, then got Oglivie to hit a high chopper over the mound. Ozzie Smith raced to the second base side of the bag and made a brilliant play to nip Oglivie and end the inning.

Then came the St. Louis eighth. With Bob McClure pitching, Hernandez walked and Porter singled with one out. Pete Ladd, who had replaced the injured Rollie Fingers as the closer, came out of the pen and walked Lonnie Smith on a 3-2 count, loading the bases. Now pinch hitter Steve Braun was up. Once again Ladd had trouble finding home plate. He walked Braun on four straight pitches, forcing in the go-ahead run.

In the ninth it was Sutter and defense. The Milwaukee hitters were Molitor, Yount, and Cooper, who already had 15 hits between them. Molitor managed

Until arm problems shortened his career, reliever Bruce Sutter set the tone for the great closers who followed. The first pitcher to throw the split-fingered fastball successfully, Sutter was one of the main reasons the 1982 Cards were world champs. *(Courtesy St. Louis Cardinals)*

a single. But when he took off for second with Yount up, catcher Porter gunned him down. Sutter then retired Yount on a grounder and Cooper on a fly out. The Cards had won it, 5–4, to even the Series.

Now the scene shifted to Milwaukee. Joaquin Andujar started for the Cards against big Pete Vuckovich of the Brewers. The game quickly turned into the Willie McGee show. The rookie centerfielder hit two home runs and made a pair of sparkling catches to rob Paul Molitor and Gorman Thomas of extra-base hits to key a 6–2 St. Louis victory. Andujar pitched into the seventh, when he was hit in the leg by a line drive off the bat of Simmons. Sutter gave up a pair of runs in relief but still got the save. It was the rookie McGee, however, who was the real hero.

"Nobody ever played a better World Series game than Willie McGee did tonight," was the way Manager Herzog put it.

Dave LaPoint and Moose Haas were the Game Four starters. Again the Brewers exploded offensively, this time getting six runs in the seventh to overcome a 5–1 Cardinals lead and win, 7–5. And when Milwaukee won the fifth game, Mike Caldwell defeating Bob Forsch 6–4, Cardinal hopes were dwindling. In fact, Milwaukee got a pair of insurance runs off Sutter in the last of the eighth, making it 6–2 before the Cards pulled to 6–4 in the ninth. With the Series returning to Busch Stadium, the Cards were just one game away from elimination.

Herzog had no choice in the sixth game but to go back to rookie Stuper, while Milwaukee had money pitcher Don Sutton primed and ready. In the eyes of many this would be the best chance the Brewers had. But then the Brewers came apart. Sutton had next to nothing. His teammates made four errors. They couldn't touch rookie Stuper until they got a meaningless run in the ninth.

The Cards, meanwhile, got a pair in the second, three more in the fourth, two in the fifth, and a big six in the sixth to win the game, in a laugher, 13–1. Hernandez led the way with a pair of hits and four RBIs, while both he and Porter smacked home runs. Despite two rain delays, Stuper went the distance for the win.

"I was kind of jumpy and had to find a way to kill time," Stuper said of the rain stoppages. "But this game showed the value of throwing strikes. I was all over the place the last time, but today I felt a lot more confident."

Now it was down to a single game for the championship. Joaquin Andujar, the Cards' best pitcher, would have the ball and be opposed by Pete Vuckovich, the Brewers' top winner. It looked like a fine matchup.

"I'm sure Milwaukee feels like they're the better ballclub, and I know we feel we're better," said the Cards' Tommy Herr. "I think whichever team executes better and makes the fewer mistakes will win."

As the Cardinals took the field before the start of the game, Ozzie Smith ignited the crowd by doing a cartwheel and backflip as he reached his position at short. They were ignited again in the bottom of the fourth when the Cards did their scratch-and-claw act to push the first run of the game across the plate. Then in the top of the fifth the Brewers did it their way. Ben Oglivie hit Andujar's first pitch into the lower deck in right, and the game was tied at 1–1.

In the sixth it seemed to come apart for the Cardinals. A Jim Gantner double, throwing error by

Andujar, bunt single by Molitor, sacrifice fly by Cooper, and Robin Yount's 12th hit of the Series gave the Brewers a pair of runs and a 3–1 lead. Now the fans were quiet. Their ballclub was in trouble, and they knew it.

But as they had done all year, these Cards didn't quit. Though Vuckovich was throwing a strong game, St. Louis went right to work on him in the bottom of the sixth. With one out, Ozzie Smith singled, and then Lonnie Smith whacked a double. Out went Vuckovich and in came left-hander Bob McClure. When veteran Gene Tenace came out to bat for Oberkfell, Kuenn ordered him walked intentionally, loading the bases.

Now Keith Hernandez was up. It didn't bother Hernandez that he was facing a lefty. In clutch situations he felt he could hit anybody. He promptly lined a base hit, scoring both Smiths with the tying runs. Seconds later George Hendrick singled home pinch runner Mike Ramsey with the third run of the inning. The Cardinals had a 4–3 lead.

Despite his sore leg, Andujar pitched through the seventh inning before giving way to Sutter in the top of the eighth. Now the Cards were going for the win, and they had their main man on the mound to do it for them. But even the ace reliever must have welcomed the help he got in the bottom of the eighth.

Run-scoring singles by Porter and Steve Braun brought home a pair of insurance runs that made the score 6–3. Minutes later Sutter fanned Gorman Thomas on a 3-2 pitch to end the game and the Series. The Cardinals were world champions once again.

It was an unlikely bunch of world champions, a

team that had only 67 home runs all year. This description by veteran baseball writer Maury Allen probably caught a good deal of the essence that was the 1982 Cardinals:

"This is Whitey's team, his creation, a bunch of rabbits who hit singles and doubles and play good defense for an underrated bunch of pitchers."

What made this ballclub into a Super Team for at least one year was their attitude and character. That can best be explained by a simple statement his teammates overheard pitcher Andujar repeating before the seventh and deciding game.

"There's no way I let these guys beat me," the Dominican pitcher said. "I die first."

1986

NEW YORK METS

It was a team that started out being a laughingstock. Seven years later, however, it pulled off one of baseball's greatest miracles, becoming a Super Team for one glorious season. Then 17 years after that, in 1986, this same ballclub was once again in the World Series. This time they were expected to win, but to do it, they had to rally from being just one strike away from losing the Series in six games. But they persevered, winning the game and the next day the championship. It was one of the great comebacks in World Series history.

The team was the New York Mets, an expansion ballclub in 1962 and one whose history is dotted with more ups and downs than a yo-yo. When they began to play in 1962, they quickly became the most futile expansion club in baseball history. The club was 40-120 their first season, a record that prompted their manager, the colorful Casey Stengel, to proclaim:

"Can't anyone here play this game!"

The Mets didn't play the game very well for five years. During each of four years the team lost more than 100 games. When they crept up to ninth in 1968, finishing with a 73-89 record under Manager Gil Hodges, no one thought too much about it. That was why 1969 became the year of the miracle. The New Yorkers won 100 games, a National League pennant, and a world championship when they upset the powerful Baltimore Orioles in just five games.

It was truly an amazing season, but the team did have talent. It started with two of the best young pitchers in the majors—Tom Seaver and Jerry Koosman—and went from there. Manager Hodges platooned a number of his players, and most of the moves he made worked. But while the 1969 Mets may have caught the proverbial lightning in a bottle, they were not really a Super Team. They were just 83-79 the next two years and took another pennant in 1973 with a very mediocre 82-79 record in divisional play and an upset win over tough Cincinnati in the playoffs. That year they lost to the Oakland A's in a seven-game World Series.

By 1977 the ballclub was back at the bottom, losing 98 games and bringing back the abysmal memories of early expansion. It wasn't until the mid-1980s that the ballclub began again reversing its fortunes. When Davey Johnson took over the managerial reins in 1984, the club suddenly improved from 68-94 to 90-72 and a second place finish. Johnson already had many of the pieces in place that would culminate in the Mets' most fantastic season ever, 1986.

The resurgence actually began in 1983. On June 15 the Mets made a major trade with the St. Louis Cardinals, acquiring first baseman Keith Hernandez, a former National League batting champ and Most Valuable Player, who was also considered one of the finest fielding first sackers in baseball history. Hernandez was not only a major talent, but he was also a leader and just 29 years old at the time of the trade.

A second major move that year involved a 21-year-old rookie slugger named Darryl Strawberry. Strawberry was the Mets' number-one draft choice in June 1980 and had been cutting a path through the minors since then. After being called up from Triple A in May, Strawberry struggled briefly, then emerged to become National League Rookie of the Year with 26 home runs, 74 RBIs, and a .257 average. In the eyes of most, he was just scratching the surface of his potential.

In 1984 the team had itself another gem, a 19-year-old right-hander with a blazing fastball and curve that broke off a table. His name was Dwight Gooden, and he was coming off a 19-4 year at Lynchburg in A ball. Gooden quickly showed he was ready for the majors and would follow Strawberry as Rookie of the Year with a 17-9 record, 276 strikeouts, and a 2.60 ERA.

The team was also gathering other young players like centerfielder Mookie Wilson, second baseman Wally Backman, and pitcher Ron Darling. A late-season trade brought veteran Ray Knight to the ballclub. He was another leader, both by example and by his outspokenness. The new, improved Mets surprised everyone with their 90-72 record, the second best mark in franchise history.

By 1985 the team was still taking shape. Another major trade brought All-Star catcher Gary Carter down from Montreal in exchange for Hubie Brooks and Mike Fitzgerald. Like Hernandez, Carter was an outstanding talent who could inspire the younger players. Third sacker Howard Johnson also joined the team, as did a scrappy outfielder named Len Dykstra. Young pitchers Roger McDowell and Rick Aguilera also showed promise, as did hard-throwing left Sid Fernandez.

The 1985 Mets battled the Cardinals until the second-to-last day of the season, when they were eliminated. But they finished with a 98-64 record, just three games back. Gooden was the big story with a 24-4 record and a Cy Young Award. The young righty had 268 strikeouts and an amazing 1.53 earned run average. But he had plenty of help. Darling won 16, Carter had 32 homers and 100 RIBs, Hernandez batted .309 with 91 ribbies. And despite missing seven full weeks with an injury, Strawberry still managed 29 homers and 79 RBIs. There were those who felt the Mets were putting together a Super Team at last.

It was no surprise, then, that the ballclub was favored to win the N.L. East in 1986. Another trade added lefty Bob Ojeda to the starting rotation. He would join Gooden, Darling, Fernandez, and Aguilera to form perhaps the finest group of starters in the majors. In fact, for the first time in the history of the franchise (including the 1969 world champs), the Mets were a solid team at every position. The bench was deep and the role players outstanding. Roger McDowell and Jesse Orosco were a righty-lefty pair of closers in the pen. There didn't seem to be a single weakness, top to bottom, on the entire ballclub.

Once the season began, it quickly became apparent that the Mets were the class of the National League. In fact, they were being called the best team in all of baseball by many of the writers, reporters, fans, and media people who covered and observed action throughout the majors. The ballclub had a perfect blend of veterans and youngsters, as well as a great pitching staff. In addition, they stayed healthy and relatively injury free.

The New Yorkers came out of the gate fast and never looked back. They played like a true Super Team from the beginning. By the All-Star break the division race was theirs. And when they lengthened their lead to a full 22 games on September 10, that was the biggest lead any team had had since divisional play began back in 1969, the year the Miracle Mets won the World Series. Fans flocked through the turnstiles at Shea Stadium to watch a team that was proving it knew how to win.

There was no dramatic story to the regular season. The Mets simply romped home winners, finishing with a great 108-54 record and winning their division by 21½ games. Almost everyone on the team put together solid seasons. Backman hit .320 in just 387 at bats, as he was platooned with Tim Teufel at second. Hernandez hit .310 with 13 homers and 83 RBIs. Carter had 105 ribbies to go with his 24 home runs. Darryl Strawberry led the club with 27 dingers, and drove home 93. Even Ray Knight, who split time with Howard Johnson, had 11 homers and 76 RBIs.

All the starting pitchers were winners. Gooden didn't duplicate that fantastic 1985 season, but was still 17-6 with 200 strikeouts. Ojeda was 18-5 in his first National League season, while Fernandez finished at 16-6 and equaled Gooden's 200 K's. Darling was 15-7 and Aguilera 10-7. In the pen, McDowell and Orosco had 43 saves and 22 wins between them. Who could ask for anything more?

After such a dominating season, the Mets were installed as nearly overwhelming favorites to advance through the playoffs and into the World Series, at which time they would undoubtedly be overwhelming favorites again. But this was where the real story of the 1986 season suddenly developed. The Mets would find themselves in a pair of battles that would test their mettle and make them prove once again that they were indeed a Super Team.

The playoffs were now a best-of-seven series, and the Mets would be meeting a team that had always been tough on them, the Houston Astros. Coincidentally, the Astros (then called the Colt 45s) were also an expansion team in 1962 when the Mets were born. Houston won 96 games in taking the N.L. West, 12 games fewer than the New Yorkers, but they had a ballclub that could give the Mets trouble.

Pitching was the Astros' strong point, and they were led by a pair of former Mets, Nolan Ryan—still tough at 39—and Mike Scott, who had emerged as an 18-8 pitcher in 1985 and was coming into the playoffs in 1986 with an 18-10 record and 306 strikeouts. He would win the Cy Young Award after the season. Lefties Jim Deshaies and Bob Knepper also pitched well against the Mets.

The Mets had to travel to the Astrodome in Houston for the opener. They had Dwight Gooden ready, and the man called the Doctor, or Doc, was almost equal to Scott—almost. Houston's Glenn Davis smacked a home run leading off the second and it turned out to be the only run of the game. Scott was brilliant. He baffled the Mets on five hits while fanning 14, including Hernandez and Carter three times each.

As lefty Bob Ojeda prepared to face Nolan Ryan in Game Two, the Mets' Wally Backman expressed the feelings of many of his teammates.

"I can live being down 1–0, especially in a best-of-seven series," Backman said. "But if we don't beat Nolan, then it's going to be very tough on us. No one wants to go home down 2–0."

So the Mets were faced with their first important game of the playoffs, and they came through. They scored two in the fourth and three in the fifth to knock out Ryan and go on to an easy 5–1 victory. Ojeda went the distance. Now it was back to Shea Stadium for the third contest with Ron Darling set to work for the Mets against southpaw Bob Knepper of the Astros.

This was another game that tested the character of the New Yorkers. Houston jumped on top, 4–0, after just two innings. Not only would a loss drop the Mets a game behind, but they were well aware that Mike Scott would be pitching again the next day. Knepper held the Mets until the bottom of the sixth. That was when the New Yorkers tied it, the key blow being a Darryl Strawberry three-run homer.

Rick Aguilera was on the hill in the top of the seventh when Houston pushed across a single run to grab the lead back at 5–4. It was still a one-run game in the bottom of the ninth. The Mets had just three outs left and were facing Houston closer Dave Smith.

Wally Backman led off and smacked a solid single. Backman then took second on a passed ball before pinch swinger Danny Heep flied to center for out number one. That brought up leadoff hitter Len Dykstra.

Though not known as a home-run hitter, Dykstra got his pitch and swung from the heels. The ball sailed into the right field stands for a dramatic, game-winning homer. The crowd went wild as Dykstra circled the bases and gave the Mets a 2-1 lead in the Series.

With a slight cushion the Mets decided to throw lefty Sid Fernandez and give Doc Gooden an extra day of rest. Although Mike Scott was going on just three days' rest, he was almost as brilliant as in the opener. This time he handcuffed the Mets on just three hits as the 'Stros won it, 3–1, to even the play-offs at two games each. Scott fanned five this time and may not have been as overpowering, but he was still nearly unhittable.

There was little doubt that Scott had the Mets worried. His late success was because of his split-fingered fastball, though the Mets and some other teams claimed he was scuffing the ball.

"I saw six balls he scuffed all over the place," said Keith Hernandez. "But we couldn't catch him doing it."

There was also the specter of Scott pitching again if the Series went to a seventh and deciding game. This was something the Mets wanted desperately to avoid, though at first they wouldn't admit it.

"If there is a Game Seven, we'll beat him," said Wally Backman. "He can't beat us three times."

But the best way to avoid that was for the Mets to win Games Five and Six. That was the objective as Doc Gooden took to the hill against Nolan Ryan. This time the two fireballers both had it. In fact, Ryan was the more overpowering of the two. Houston pushed across a run in the top of the fifth before Strawberry tied it with a solo shot in the bottom of the inning.

It was still that way after nine, a 1–1 game as Ryan had fanned 12 and retired the final seven Mets he faced after walking Strawberry in the seventh. But reliever Charlie Kerfeld replaced Ryan in the tenth, and Gooden gave way to Jesse Orosco in the eleventh. It was still tied at 1–1 as the game went to the 12th. Once again the Mets were facing almost a *must* game. And once again it was Wally Backman who got things started, legging out an infield hit.

When Kerfeld tried to pick him off first, Backman scooted down to second. The Astros then walked Hernandez intentionally, setting up a potential double play. Now Gary Carter was up. Carter was mired in a playoff slump that saw him with just a single hit in 21 trips to the plate. But this time the Mets catcher came through, slamming a base hit to drive Backman home with the winning run. The New Yorkers would now be returning to Houston with a 3–2 lead in games.

But the pressure was still on. If they didn't win Game Six, it would be Scott again in the seventh. So as Bob Ojeda took the hill against Bob Knepper, there was still a lot at stake. This was a game that turned into a classic and helped to create the image of the 1986 Mets as a Super Team. It started when Houston scored three first-inning runs to take an early lead. Ojeda then settled down, but the Mets could do nothing against Knepper, who was keeping them off-balance with his curves and off-speed pitches. Going to the top of the ninth, the Astros were still holding to that 3–0 lead.

Catcher Gary Carter joined the Mets after a great career in Montreal and immediately made an impact with the New Yorkers. Carter's work behind the plate and clutch bat were one of the big reasons the Mets became baseball's best in 1986. *(Courtesy New York Mets)*

As usual, the Mets didn't quit. Pinch hitter Dykstra opened with a big triple to deep center. When Mookie Wilson followed with a single, the Mets had their first run. After a groundout that sent Wilson to second, Keith Hernandez was up. Once again Hernandez delivered in the clutch, this time slamming a double that drove Wilson home with run number two. Dave Smith came on to walk both Hernandez and Strawberry, loading the bases. When Ray Knight cracked a long sacrifice fly, the game was tied at 3–3. From there it went to extra innings. That was when it became a battle.

Neither team scored for the next four innings, but in the 14th Backman drove in the go-ahead run with a base hit. In the bottom of the inning, however, Houston's Billy Hatcher smacked a home run off Roger McDowell and the game was tied again, this time at 4–4. In the 16th a Strawberry double, a Knight single, a pair of wild pitches sandwiched around a walk, a sacrifice, and a Dykstra single gave the Mets three runs and a 7–4 lead.

Now Jesse Orosco tried to close it out. But a one-out walk and a Bill Doran single put two 'Stros on base. When Hatcher slammed a single, Houston had one back. A fielder's choice and single by Davis made it 7–6. Now Kevin Bass was up with two on and two out, the game and playoffs on the line. Orosco bore down and fanned Bass. It was finally over. The Mets had won in 16, 7–6. They took the Series 4–2 and would move on to the World Series. And they wouldn't have to face Mike Scott again.

"If we had to face Scott tomorrow, I might not have slept tonight," said one Met.

"This is my 16th year in professional baseball, and

I've never been a part of anything so emotional and so draining," said Ray Knight. "Every play was critical. Every pitch . . . was a one-on-one confrontation, and every at bat was a critical at bat."

But it wasn't over yet. The Mets still had the World Series looming, and their opponents would be the Boston Red Sox, a team that rallied from a 3–1 deficit to defeat the California Angels in the American League playoffs. The Bosox were a powerful and balanced team. Their star pitcher, Roger Clemens, had equaled Dwight Gooden's 1985 season by going 24-4. He had solid help from lefty Bruce Hurst and right-hander Dennis "Oil Can" Boyd.

At the plate the Sox boasted four top hitters—Jim Rice, Bill Buckner, Dwight Evans, and Don Baylor. The first two topped the 100 RBI mark, while the last two had 97 and 94 ribbies respectively. Add American League batting champ Wade Boggs (.357) and it was easy to see why the Sox were so good. The only place the Mets seemed to have an advantage was in the bullpen and in overall team speed.

It would be a kind of odd Series in that the bulk of the drama and excitement was packed into the final games. Not that the beginning was dull. The games were hard-fought but simply lacked the little extra that keeps fans on pins and needles. Coincidentally, the first game was almost a carbon-copy of the first Mets-Astros playoff game. New York went with Ron Darling while the Red Sox countered with lefty Bruce Hurst. A cheering throng of 55,076 fans jammed Shea Stadium for the opener.

Both pitchers were razor sharp and throwing nothing but goose eggs. Then, in the seventh, it was the Mets who faltered. A Tim Teufel error at second allowed the Sox to score the only run of the game. Hurst scattered four hits in eight innings, while Calvin Schiraldi worked the ninth to record the save. Next came the so-called dream matchup, the meeting of right-handers Doc Gooden and Roger Clemens. Both Gooden and Clemens said it wasn't a personal thing.

"It's a big game because it's the World Series," said Gooden. "I can't worry about Clemens. I let the hitters do that."

Same with Roger. "I'm sure it's what everybody has been waiting for. But I'm facing the Mets hitters. It's not me against Dwight."

As it turned out, the anticipation was much greater than the reality. Neither superstar pitcher had his good stuff. Gooden lasted just five innings and gave up six runs. Clemens was relieved after just $4\frac{1}{3}$ innings, giving up three runs. The difference was that the Sox bullpen did the job, the Mets' didn't. Boston wound up rapping out 18 hits and winning, 9–3. They had taken both games at Shea and were returning to the friendly confines of ancient Fenway Park with a 2–0 lead in the Series. And once again the Mets found themselves facing what amounted to a *must* game.

As Ron Darling said, "We have to turn it around. I'm not panicking, but if we go down 3–0 and have two more games left at Fenway, we're close to being done."

That seemed to be the prevailing sentiment as lefty Bob Ojeda, a former Red Sox, took the mound against Oil Can Boyd. As he had in the playoffs, Ojeda pitched the Mets back into the Series. He had first-inning help from his hitters. Dykstra went downtown again, leading off the game with a home run.

Backman and Hernandez followed with singles. Then Carter doubled home Backman, and before the inning ended Danny Heep had singled in Hernandez. That gave the Mets a 4–0 lead before all the Red Sox fans had even reached their seats.

From there Ojeda cruised. The veteran left-hander scattered five hits and allowed just one run in seven innings. Roger McDowell pitched the final two frames for the save. The New Yorkers were still in it but needed Game Four to tie things up and reclaim a possible home field advantage. Ron Darling would be coming back on three days' rest, but the Sox decided to gamble, using Al Nipper as a fourth starter.

The gamble backfired. Carter hit a two-run homer in the fourth, and Knight singled in a third run. By the eighth inning the Mets had a 6–0 lead as Dykstra and Carter again added homers. Darling went seven scoreless frames before McDowell gave up a pair in the eighth and Orosco had to put out the fire. The 6–2 final had squared the Series at two games each.

Gooden and Bruce Hurst were the fifth-game starters. The Doctor yielded four runs in five innings before Sid Fernandez came to the rescue. Hurst, meanwhile, pitched his second strong game and emerged with a 4–2 victory. So with the Series returning to Shea for a sixth game, the Mets were again in an all-too-familiar post-season position. It was *must win* time again, and standing in the New Yorkers' way was Roger Clemens, the best pitcher in baseball.

Bob Ojeda was again asked to pitch the Mets back in it, but when the Sox got single runs in both the first and second, Mets fans had plenty of reason to worry. Especially when Clemens had come out of the gate looking very sharp. When the Mets came to bat in the bottom of the fifth, they still trailed, 2–0, and didn't have a single hit.

But a walk to Strawberry, a stolen base, and a Ray Knight single made it a 2–1 game. A Mookie Wilson single to right sent Knight to third, and he scored when Danny Heep hit into a 4–6–3 double play. Now the game was tied, and it stayed that way until the top of the seventh. With McDowell pitching for the Mets the Red Sox pushed across the go-ahead run and had moved within nine outs of a world championship.

Clemens retired the Mets in the seventh, then left in favor of Calvin Schiraldi, who was on the mound to begin the eighth. Lee Mazzilli started things with a base hit and minutes later scored from third on a sacrifice fly by Carter. It stayed 3–3 right through the ninth, and the two teams went to extra innings. Rick Aguilera was on the hill for the Mets and was touched for three hits and two runs in the top of the 10th, one of them coming in courtesy of a Dave Henderson homer. As the Mets came up in the bottom of the tenth, they trailed by two, 5–3, and a feeling a gloom settled over Shea Stadium.

It got even worse when Schiraldi retired the first two Mets on routine fly balls. Now the New Yorkers, the team that won 108 games during the regular season, were down to their final out. Gary Carter was up and Schiraldi got two strikes on him, putting the Mets just a strike away from a devastating defeat. All the while Carter kept thinking to himself:

"I'm not going to make the final out of the World Series!"

Sure enough, the All-Star catcher fought off Schiraldi and rapped a base hit to left. Now rookie Kevin Mitchell stepped up as a pinch hitter. What a spot to be in. But Mitchell singled to center, sending Carter to second. Now the fans were stirring around as Ray Knight stepped up. Knight promptly slammed a single to center, scoring Carter and sending Mitchell to third. It as now a 5–4 game. Exit Schiraldi—enter veteran Bob Stanley. Switch-hitter Mookie Wilson was up, standing in on the left side against Stanley.

Stanley tried to be too fine and threw a low, inside pitch. The acrobatic Wilson jumped and twisted out of the way, and the ball missed him and also catcher Rich Gedman. Mitchell sprinted home on the wild pitch, and the game was tied. Shea Stadium erupted as Wilson stepped back in. Again the battle continued, Stanley and Wilson. Finally Mookie hit a weak grounder toward first. Bill Buckner came over to field it—but it went through his legs. The Mets bench erupted as Knight sprinted home with the winning run! Incredibly, the Mets had pulled it out, 6–5, coming back from the depths of the defeated. They were one strike away. Now they had forced a seventh and deciding game.

"Just goes to show you, if you keep fighting, anything can happen," said a jubilant Knight after the game.

But it wasn't over yet. Darling and Hurst hooked up again in the seventh game, and once again the Mets found themselves behind. Three Sox runs in the second saw to that. Hurst held the New Yorkers scoreless until the bottom of the sixth. Still trailing by that same 3–0 margin, the Mets went to work. With one out, base hits by Mazzilli and Wilson, fol-

Keith Hernandez provided the same spark with the Mets that he had given the Cardinals. The slick-fielding first baseman was a role model for the younger players and is still one of the great clutch hitters in the game. *(Courtesy New York Mets)*

lowed by a walk to Teufel loaded the bases. Keith Hernandez was next, and he came through in the clutch again, singling home two runs. Carter then bounced into a fielder's choice, but it was good enough to get the tying run across the plate.

With the excitement mounting, the Mets came up against Calvin Schiraldi in the bottom of the seventh. The fiery Ray Knight started it by blasting a long home run to center field. For the first time in the playoffs and Series, the Mets were in the driver's seat. They must have liked it, because a single by Dykstra, a wild pitch and single by Rafael Santana got another run home. Then a sacrifice fly by Hernandez brought the third run in. It was 6–3.

Two Sox runs in the eighth made it 6–5, but the Mets were not to be denied. In the bottom of the inning they got two more, one of them coming on a titanic homer by Strawberry. It was now 8–5, and there were no more miracles left for the Red Sox. Jesse Orosco closed them out, and the Mets were champions.

What a battle it had been. After cruising through the regular season in dominating fashion, the ballclub had to fight and scrap right through the postseason and almost to the final inning.

"It doesn't get any better than this," cooed Manager Davey Johnson when it was over. "This is what it's all about."

Johnson was right. It doesn't get better, and it didn't get better. Though deep and talented, the Mets never repeated their 1986 success. They won 100 games and another divisional crown in 1988 but were upset in the playoffs by the Dodgers. Whatever had clicked in 1986 wasn't there anymore. Some felt the club had let too many scrappers go, guys like Knight and Backman, role players and leaders. Others felt that age had caught up to vets like Hernandez and Carter, and that injuries may have played a role.

Whatever the reason, the 1986 season was special. The New York Mets were a very good baseball team for a period of six or seven years. But for one fantastic season, 1986, they were a Super Team. Just ask any opponent who thought they had the Mets beaten.

1989

OAKLAND A'S

They were a team that couldn't be stopped, not even by a tragic earthquake minutes before the start of the third game of the World Series. They had poise and power, pitching, speed, defense, and superstars and near-superstars at a number of positions. They had the best closer in baseball as well as perhaps the best leadoff hitter in the history of the game. They were the 1989 Oakland A's, and if the ingredients for a Super Team were ever in place, the A's were in possession of nearly all of them.

The A's had something of a legacy. After moving from Kansas City to Oakland in the late 1960s, the team built itself into a champion, winning five straight A.L. West titles and three consecutive world championships between 1971 and 1974. These were the A's of Reggie Jackson, Catfish Hunter, Sal Bando, Vida Blue, Joe Rudi, Rollie Fingers, and Bert Campaneris among others. They were a Super Team who knew how to win when the chips were down.

But owner Charles O. Finley squabbled with many of his star players, and it resulted in their slowly leaving, plunging the team downward. Finley finally sold the ballclub, and the new owners began rebuilding. Yet, except for a couple of years in the early 1980s, losing records continued through 1986, when the club finished at 76-86. But by the end of the season, Tony LaRussa had taken over as manager and the club was beginning to gather some fine young players. Rookie Jose Canseco smashed 33 homers and drove home 117 runs. Right-hander Dave Stewart joined the rotation and won 9 games. Third sacker Carney Lansford stabilized the infield. It led to an 81-81 season in 1987.

That year the slugging Canseco was joined by rookie first sacker Mark McGwire, who set a first year record by blasting 49 home runs. He also drove in 118 and was joined by Canseco with 31 homers and 113 ribbies. The team had a dominating pair of young sluggers. Lansford had 19 homers, while Terry Steinbach took over behind the plate and slammed 16. On the hill Stewart became a 20-game winner and veteran Dennis Eckersley began establishing himself as a premier closer.

But that still didn't prepare anyone for what happened in 1988. The A's added a few more key players and came of age, to the tune of 104 victories and an American League pennant. Though they were upset in the World Series by the Dodgers in five games, no one doubted that the Oakland A's were for real.

Canseco was the MVP in 1988 with a league best 42 homers and 124 RBIs. He also hit .307 and swiped 40 bases. McGwire whacked 32 homers, while the newly acquired Dave Henderson had 24. Rookie Walt Weiss was a Rookie of the Year shortstop, while veterans like Dave Parker and Don Baylor added a world of experience. Stewart won 21, while Bob Welch and Storm Davis took 17 and 16 respectively. Eckersley was untouchable with 45 big saves. With all this firepower the A's were considered solid favorites at the outset of the 1989 campaign.

"Sure, we had the best team last year in just about every way you could measure," Manager LaRussa said. "We met and passed every test—well, except one."

That one was the World Series. So the A's felt they had something to prove. Even the players felt it.

"There's no reason we can't be back in the Series this year, next year, and the following year," said Canseco.

Mark McGwire added, "We were too eager, too impatient in the Series last year, and the Dodgers took advantage of that. I think we've all profited from that experience."

Time would tell. Before the season opened, the team added yet another quality starter, signing free agent right-hander Mike Moore from Seattle. It soon became apparent that the A's would need all their resources just to repeat as American League West champions. The problem was injury. Super slugger Canseco injured a wrist in spring training and would miss virtually the entire first half of the season. Then, shortly after the season began, McGwire went on the disabled list with a less serious injury. So the team played nearly the entire month of April without the "Bash Brothers," as the two had come to be called. Yet instead of folding, the A's were 9-4 in games when both Canseco and McGwire were missing.

Slugger Mark McGwire was one of the mainstays of the 1989 A's. The big first sacker set a record with 49 homers in his 1987 rookie year and continued his slugging when the A's became world champs. *(Courtesy Oakland Athletics)*

"In a way, I think it was easier for LaRussa to manage when both of those sluggers were out," said California Angels manager Doug Rader. "The ballclub provided Tony with a nice bunch of role players, and they went from the power game to the running game. And they were very successful."

Then in May the club suffered yet another blow when shortstop Walt Weiss, already the leader in the infield, hurt a knee and would be out until August. Thanks to the pitching and the role players, the team continued to play winning baseball, but they weren't dominating. Both the Angels and the Kansas City Royals were hanging close.

A's management felt the team needed a spark, something to ignite it. Maybe another quality player. Suddenly there was a potential deal staring right at Oakland management. It was something they couldn't turn down, and on June 21 they pulled the trigger. The news made headlines on sports pages all across the country.

The A's had lost superstar Rickey Henderson to the New York Yankees following the 1984 season. Henderson was the game's premier leadoff man, capable of generating home-run power as well as being the best stolen base man in the majors. By 1984 he had already set the single-season mark of 130 steals and would eventually become baseball's all-time base thief during the 1991 season.

Henderson had gone to the Yanks as a free agent but in 1989 had fallen into disfavor with New York Yankee management. He was also disenchanted playing for mediocre Yankee teams and often performed as if he had a case of the blahs. So the Yanks dealt him back to the A's for left fielder Luis Polonia and a pair of relief pitchers, Eric Plunk, and Greg Cadaret. Once "back home" in Oakland, Henderson began doing his thing. And when he did it right, he did it better than any player in baseball.

Henderson provided the anticipated spark and helped make up for the loss of Canseco. He was still the old Rickey, capable of leading off a game with a homer or creating havoc on the base paths. No more blahs. As soon as he returned to Oakland, Henderson performed like an All-Star again.

By the end of August the race was still close, but the scales were tipping in favor of the A's. On the 27th of the month the A's had a 79-52 mark. California was next at 77-52, while the Royals were in striking distance with a record of 75-55. In other words, the division was still there for the taking. But most experts favored the A's.

The pitching was holding up beautifully. Stewart had already won 17, Moore 16, Welch and Davis 14 each. And Eckersley was better than ever. Though missing some 40 games himself because of injury, he had saved 27 and had a microscopic 0.95 earned run average. When he came in to close out a game, it was almost an automatic.

Both Lansford and Steinbach were having fine seasons. Henderson had 60 steals; designated hitter Parker had 17 homers and 71 RBIs. Though hitting just .234, McGwire led the club with 24 homers and 76 ribbies. And there was an indication that Canseco was starting to find the range. The big slugger had played in just 34 games through August 24, but he had 7 homers and 24 RBIs. The injured wrist, he said, was feeling better every day.

As the team moved into the September shootout,

it was healthier than at any previous time during the season. It was soon apparent that at full strength, the Oakland A's were still the class of the division, a ballclub with more than enough talent to cross the line and become a real Super Team. Finally, on September 27, the A's went up against the Texas Rangers. If they won, they'd clinch the division title for a second straight year.

With Mike Moore on the mound and going after his 19th win, the A's went to work. They showed all the elements. Canseco hit a huge, two-run homer. The defense turned three slick double plays. Moore faced the minimum 21 hitters while pitching seven innings of one-run ball before the bullpen took over. The final was 5–0, and the A's were champions once again. it was a title that everyone really seemed to appreciate and savor.

"It was a tough ordeal, but we survived it," said Dave Parker. "Last year we just beat up on people. This year we fought, we scratched, and we hung in there."

Manager LaRussa echoed those thoughts. "Carney Lansford, Dave Henderson, Parker, the catchers, Tony Phillips—these guys really had to grind through the first half," LaRussa said. "The second half was more fair because we had help."

"This was a long road," said Canseco, who had to battle back from injury. "Both [division titles] felt pretty good, but there were different circumstances. This year, we had to fight."

Though they won five games fewer than in 1988, the A's nevertheless finished with the best record in baseball at 99-63. They topped the Royals by seven games and the Angels by eight. Now the ballclub looked forward to the postseason. They wanted to win very badly, not only for themselves but for their growing number of fans. Unlike the great Oakland teams of the early 1970s that had trouble drawing a million fans, these A's had caught the public fancy. In 1989 the team drew a record 2,667,225 fans, including a franchise best 19 sellouts, at the Oakland Coliseum.

Individually, there were outstanding seasons. Lansford was the team's leading hitter at .336. Parker led in RBIs with 97, adding 22 home runs. McGwire walloped 33 and drove home 95 runs, while Canseco finished with 17 homers and 57 RBIs in just 227 at bats, less than half a season. Rickey Henderson hit .294 with Oakland after hitting just .247 with the Yanks. He also hit 9 of his 12 homers with the A's and drove in 35 of his 57 runs after returning to Oakland. His two-team totals enabled him to lead the league in runs scored (113), walks (126), and stolen bases (77). Dave Henderson added 15 homers and 80 RBIs.

On the hill Stewart finished at 21-9, Moore at 19-11, Welch at 17-8, and Davis at 19-7. That's a big four that would be tough to beat. The middle relievers— Gene Nelson, Todd Burns, and Rick Honeycutt—all filled their roles, while Eckersley had a 4-0 record, 33 saves, and a 1.56 ERA. On paper the A's were still the best.

Practically speaking, they still had to prove it on the field. Standing in their way first were the Toronto Blue Jays, who had taken the A.L. East with an 89-73 mark, not a real super performance. But Toronto had good power with American League homer champ Fred McGriff (36 homers, 92 RBIs), George Bell (18,

A good but not great starter early in his career, Denni
Eckersley became a superstar as a short reliever with the A's
As the team's closer, he used impeccable control and a still
smoking fastball to become nearly unhittable in ninth-inning
game-saving situations. *(Courtesy Oakland Athletics)*

04), and Kelly Gruber (18, 73). Tony Fernandez was considered one of the best shortstops in baseball.

On the other hand, the starting pitching boasted just one guy with a winning record, Dave Steib at 17-. John Cerutti was 11-11, Jimmy Key 13-14, Mike Flanagan 8-10, and Todd Stottlemyre 7-7. The bullpen trio of Duane Ward, Tom Henke, and David Wells was outstanding, taking a lot of heat off the starters. But it was apparent that the A's had the better, all-round ballclub.

A pair of Daves, Stewart and Stieb, were the starting pitchers in Game One of the American League playoffs, a best-of-seven series. And the first game would clearly set the tone for what would follow. Toronto surprisingly took a 3–1 lead over Stewart and the A's after four innings. But Oakland battled back, getting a run in the fifth, three in the sixth, and two in the eighth to wind up with a decisive, 7–3, victory.

It was the three in the sixth, however, that showed major difference in the 1989 A's. The first came on a Mark McGwire homer. But it was Rickey Henderson's ability to upend Toronto second sacker Nelson Liriano and cause a wild throw that allowed the next two to score.

"The only guy in the league who could have got to me fast enough to make that happen is Rickey Henderson," said Liriano.

In the second game Mike Moore pitched the A's to a 6–3 victory, the team scoring five unanswered runs in the fourth and sixth after Toronto had taken 1–0 lead. In that contest Henderson swiped four bases and scored two runs. Toronto managed to win the third game, 7–3, behind Jimmy Key, but Oakland took the fourth game, 6–5, as Rickey Henderson hit a pair of homers and drove home four runs. He was totally dominating the playoffs.

With the A's up, three games to one, Dave Stewart went out to try to wrap it up. In this one Henderson's steal of second in the first inning set up the first Oakland run. Two innings later, he blasted a long triple off Dave Stieb to drive in Walt Weiss with the second run. The A's built a 2–0 lead within three, then increased it to a 4–0 in the seventh. Though the Blue Jays came back with one in the eighth and two in the ninth, it wasn't enough. The A's were champions again and headed back to the World Series.

Rickey Henderson had put on a great show, setting a playoff record with eight stolen bases. For his efforts he was named the MVP. Even his manager was impressed.

"I don't think the series Rickey had against Toronto can be topped," the A's manager said. "He has all the abilities, and he brings them to the park and uses them every day."

But Henderson wasn't the only reason the A's had repeated as A.L. champs. Centerfielder Dave Henderson, who had played with the A.L. champ Red Sox in 1986, said the A's were a much deeper ballclub.

"It takes 24 players," Henderson said. "That Boston team had about 10 players and six pitchers. The depth wasn't there, but it is here."

Now the A's were ready for the final hurdle, the World Series. They would be facing the San Francisco Giants, a team that seemed to be maturing ahead of schedule. The Giants were third in the N.L. West in 1988 with an 83-79 record, but just 4½ games behind division-winning Cincinnati. In 1989 the

Giants improved their record to 92-70 and won the division by three games over San Diego.

Some thought they had done it with mirrors. The ballclub didn't have strong starting pitching, but they had a manager in Roger Craig who was a master at manipulating his hurlers. They had a pair of fine relievers in lefty Craig Lefferts and righty Steve Bedrosian who had 37 saves between them. Veteran Rick Reuschel was the top winner at 17-8, while Scott Garrelts checked in at 14-5. Don Robinson (12-11) and Mike LaCoss (10-10) were up and down.

The strength of the team was its hitting, especially the one-two punch of Kevin Mitchell and Will Clark. Mitchell would be the National League's Most Valuable Player after leading the league with 47 homers and 125 RBIs to go with his .291 batting average. Clark hit a scalding .333 and added 23 homers with 111 RBIs. Second baseman Robby Thompson and third sacker Matt Williams also showed some pop with the bat, and the club had the best slugging average in the league. In the playoffs the Giants surprised the Chicago Cubs, defeating them easily, four games to one.

But the A's were heavy favorites in the Series and showed why in the first two games, which were held in Oakland. Dave Stewart, who had completed his third straight 20-win campaign, took to the mound and stifled the Giants on just five hits. Oakland broke it open quickly. In the second inning Dave Henderson walked and came around on singles by Steinbach and Tony Phillips. Walt Weiss hit a grounder to Clark at first, who threw home only to have Steinbach kick the ball out of catcher Terry Kennedy's glove. A Rickey Henderson single brought the third run home.

Solo homers by Dave Parker in the fourth and Weiss in the fifth completed the scoring. Stewart twirled a five-hit shutout, and the A's had the lead. With Mike Moore opposing Rich Reuschel in Game Two, the scenerio was almost the same. The A's got a run in the first, then four in the fourth—a three-run homer by Steinbach the highlight. Moore went on to pitch a four-hitter with help from Rick Honeycutt and Eckersley over the last two innings. The A's won it, 5–1, and had a two-game cushion as the Series moved across the Bay to Candlestick Park in San Francisco for Game Three.

That game was scheduled to begin at 5:30 P.M. on the afternoon of October 17. At 5:04 P.M., with the ballpark jammed to capacity and both clubs getting ready, the earth began to shake without warning. Within seconds everyone in the entire Bay Area knew what was happening. A major earthquake was in progress. It was a quake that would register 6.9 on the Richter scale, the strongest quake in the Bay Area since the devasting quake of 1906.

Fortunately, there was little panic in the ballpark. Though there would be some $1 million in structural damage done to Candlestick, most of it was limited to cracks in the structure, so the packed house didn't even know at first how damaging the quake had been. After getting reports of the damage and because they had lost electrical power in the ballpark, Commissioner Fay Vincent postponed the game. Many of the players asked their families to come out of the stands to be with them to make sure they got home safely. As Dave Parker said:

"Your first reaction is to find those you love and

care for. We just wanted to make sure they were safe. And we wanted to get them out of there.''

Damage was extensive. Many homes were destroyed, a segment of the Bay Bridge collapsed into the water, and a top portion of a double-tiered highway in Oakland collapsed onto the bottom portion, killing a number of motorists. Suddenly baseball and the World Series seemed relatively unimportant. It was finally decided that there would be a 10-day break. The Series would resume with Game Three at Candlestick on October 27.

Some felt the Series should have been canceled, that the tragedy of the earthquake should not be minimized. But others felt that a return to normalcy would be best for people still shell-shocked by the terrible tremor.

"I've spoken to a lot of people," said A's pitcher Dave Stewart, "and a great majority of them are talking with enthusiasm about getting the Series started again. I think they need an [emotional] outlet."

Dave Parker added. "The tragedy was basically in Oakland. That's where most of the deaths occurred. I've got a hollow feeling about all this, and I wish we [the players] could do more. The best thing we can do is bring the championship back to our city. I think the folks in Oakland need a shot in the arm. And with two more wins maybe we can give it to them."

The Series did indeed resume on October 27. With the 10-day gap, Manager LaRussa decided to come back with Stewart and Mike Moore again as his starters, bypassing Bob Welch and Storm Davis, who would have started had there been no quake. The Giants countered with Scott Garrelts, their Game One

131

starter. It didn't take the A's long to take up right where they had left off.

With two runners on in the top of the first, Dave Henderson slammed a long liner to right. The ball bounced off the top of the railing, missing by an inch of being a three-run homer. Instead, it went into the books as a two-run double, and the A's were on the board. For a couple of innings, though, it looked as if the Giants were going to make a fight of it.

Matt Williams blasted a solo shot off Stewart in the second. And when the A's got two more in the top of the fourth, Tony Phillips and Dave Henderson hitting solo shots to knock out Garrelts, the Giants came back with two more in their half of the inning to keep it close at 4–3. But they couldn't hang with the power of the A's for long. Oakland began using the San Francisco relief pitchers for batting practice.

In the fifth they got four more, Canseco hitting a three-run blast and Dave Henderson slamming his second of the game. Carney Lansford would later hit a solo shot of his own, and in the top of the eighth the A's bunched together another four runs. That made it 13–3. Stewart had departed after seven, but when the Giants got four in the ninth off the Oakland relievers, it meant little. The final score was 13–7 and the A's had a 3-0 lead in the Series.

The fourth game was almost academic, especially when Rickey Henderson led it off with a home run off Giant starter Don Robinson. In the second, pitcher Moore became the only American League hurler in the 1980s to get a base hit when he lined a two-run double over the head of Brett Butler in center field. When Rickey Henderson singled home Moore, it was a 4–0 game. A two-run double by

Steinbach made it 6–0 in the fifth before a Tony Phillips single sent Steinbach home with run number seven. A triple by Rickey Henderson, followed by a Lansford single, made it 8–0 in the sixth.

After that the Giants fought back, getting a pair on a Mitchell homer in the sixth and four more in the seventh. The A's would get an insurance run in the eighth before Eckersley closed down the Giants, the game, and the Series in the ninth. The final score was 9–6, and the A's had swept. Not even a devastating earthquake could stop them.

So the A's had completed their mission, done the one thing they had failed to do the year before when everyone was calling them the best team in baseball. They were world champions.

"We have so many ways to win a game, but our best weapon was heart," said a happy Tony LaRussa after it ended.

"We're young and talented and most of our key players are under multiyear contracts," Mark McGwire said. "So there's no reason we can't keep winning, no reason we can't become a dynasty."

That was the magic word. Undoubtedly, the A's of 1989 were a Super Team. They had all the elements— power, pitching, speed, defense, and depth. But to call a team a dynasty, it had to win the World Series more than once. There was some inevitable comparison with the A's of the early 1970s, a ballclub that won it all three straight years.

Dave Duncan, a catcher on the 1972 team and pitching coach of the current A's, felt the 1989 team was better.

"There are a lot of similarities between the two ballclubs," said Duncan. "Both had all the elements you need to win. But I think the most dramatic thing about our current club is that it was able to win so many games over the last two regular seasons despite the fact that our league, top to bottom, has a lot more depth than it did 15 years ago. It's not easy to compare talent across generations, but I'd say about half the starters on the 1989 club could have started for those seventies Oakland teams and vice versa.''

Comparisons are difficult unless you go into great detail, and then it's still tough. A Super Team? Yes, the A's of 1989 qualify. They would also come back to win another pennant in 1990, but in the World Series were inexplicably swept by the Cincinnati Reds. And therein lies the difference.

The A's of 1972–74 won. They won despite squabbles, problems with the owner, and injuries. When push came to shove on the field, they came through. They were a Super Team and a dynasty. The A's from 1988 to 1990 did everything but win the Series in two of those years. Only the 1989 team went all the way. So while this version of the A's is surely a Super Team, they have not yet qualified as a dynasty.

1990
CINCINNATI REDS

They were unlikely champions in every way. For one
thing, they were coming off a sub-.500 season, a season in which their manager was banned from baseball
for life. During the many months in which Pete Rose
was being investigated by the commissioner's office,
the Cincinnati Reds were in turmoil. Rose was an
institution in Cincinnati, one of the all-time great players in the game as well as its all-time hit leader. He
seemed to be finding his stride as a manager when
the investigation into his gambling activities surfaced.

Coach Tommy Helms became the interim manager
for the final 35 games, and the team finished fifth in
the National League West with a 75-87 record. That
team had a superstar outfielder in Eric Davis, who
finished with 34 homers and 101 RBIs. But Davis
often had injury problems and hadn't played more
than 135 games over the previous four years.

Youngsters Paul O'Neill and Todd Benzinger showed
promise, while shortstop Barry Larkin seemed ready

to emerge as the league's best. Larkin hit .342 but was also injured and limited to 97 games. Third sacker Chris Sabo, the rookie of the year in 1988, hit just .260 and played in just 82 games because of injury. There were also too many journeymen and veterans, and the starting pitching was weak. Tom Browning was top starter at 15-12, while John Franco was the closer out of the pen with 32 saves. The club had two other fine relievers in Norm Charlton and Rob Dibble.

But that nucleus still didn't cause other teams in the division to shake with fear. Before the 1990 season began, the Reds got a new manager. He was Sweet Lou Piniella, the former skipper of the New York Yankees, and before that a hard-nosed player and intense competitor. Piniella was a well-liked boss but a guy who expected his players to work hard and compete. His appointment as manager was met with almost unanimous approval.

Otherwise, there weren't very many changes in the team. One major trade was an exchange of left-handed closers. John Franco was sent to the New York Mets for hard-throwing Randy Myers. Myers would join two other fastballers—Dibble and Charlton—in the Reds' pen. Otherwise, the team hoped the injury jinx wouldn't strike again, as it had in 1989. Two starters who saw little action were righty Jose Rijo and lefty Danny Jackson. Both were quality pitchers when healthy.

Young Joe Oliver was penciled in as the new catcher. Benzinger, Larkin, and Sabo were back at first, short, and third, while Mariano Duncan, who had come over from the Dodgers, won the second

Sweet Lou Piniella was a fiery player during an outstanding big-league career. As the first-year manager of the 1990 Cincinnati Reds, Piniella proved a fiery leader who brought out the best in his players and was rewarded with a world title. *(Courtesy Cincinnati Reds)*

base job. Davis and O'Neill were two outfield starters, while left field looked like a platoon among several players. One preseason assessment, however,
said that when healthy, "the Reds probably have the
best talent in the division."

A deadlock in player-owner negotiations caused a
lockout during spring training and a late start to the
season. But the Reds got out of the gate fast and by
the end of April had already taken the lead in the
N.L. West. Their 12-3 mark gave them a 3½ game
margin over the Dodgers, and the team began to be
noticed. Many Reds players credited their new manager with the turnaround, praising him as a teacher
whose hands-on approach was working.

"Lou is able to analyze hitting, and he can teach
you how to relate it to other things you might do,
like playing golf or tennis," said Chris Sabo. "He
can show you how you're back too far in the box, or
if you're off-balance—things like that."

The new manager also surrounded himself with
coaches who were adept at teaching the fundamentals
of the game. Just because players were major leagu-
ers didn't mean they still couldn't learn.

"Let's just say that with a young club you can
never have too many teachers," Piniella would say.
He also had the team running a lot more than it did
in the past. "I love the way this Reds team shapes
up because it can really create havoc with its speed,"
the manager continued. "I've always liked the speed
game, even though I wasn't that kind of player
myself."

By the first week in May the Reds were 17-5 and
five full games in front. The team had a hot pitcher
in right-hander Jack Armstrong, who had won his first

five starts with a 1.08 earned run average. His catcher, Joe Oliver, was also putting on a show. Oliver had thrown out 10 of the first 18 runners who tried to steal on him, a very good percentage. Expos Manager Buck Rodgers was among those impressed.

"Oliver is putting on quite a show," said Rodgers. "He gets rid of the ball with accuracy, the best I've seen in a long while."

The team seemed to be coming together. Through May 3 Duncan was hitting .377, Sabo .355, newly acquired Billy Hatcher .347, Larkin .338, Benzinger .329. Eric Davis was hitting just .186 and again was slowed by injury, but once he got the range, watch out.

By May 20 the Reds were 25-9 and had a 7½ game bulge over the Dodgers. It was beginning to look as if the team was going to run away from the division and hide. The club also had the best record in all of baseball. They were starting to attract more and more attention. One group that began to get its share of ink was the relief trio of Myers, Dibble, and Charlton. They were blowing hitters away with their smoke and enjoying it. Together they were given the nickname the "Nasty Boys."

The name referred to the high heat all three could dispense. Dibble, for instance, threw close to 100 miles per hour. His fastball had accounted for 141 strikeouts in 99 innings during the 1989 season. That averaged to a ratio of 12.8 strikeouts per nine innings, the best in modern baseball history for pitchers with 100 or more strikeouts.

Charlton, a righty, was 8-3 in 1989, pitching both long and middle relief. He was versatile enough to do everything from starting to short relief. Myers had racked up 148 saves in six years with the Mets before coming to Cincinnati. He, too, threw exceptionally hard and was known as a no-nonsense competitor on the mound. Manager Piniella didn't hesitate to go to any of the Nasty Boys when the going got tough.

Close to All-Star Game time the Reds continued to maintain a big lead. The club was 46-27 and 9½ games ahead of the defending champ Giants, who were playing just .500 ball at 38-38. There didn't seem to be a team in the division capable of catching Cincy. Sometimes when a team has a big lead, it becomes difficult to keep up the motivation. But the Reds seemed to be enjoying it.

They continued to get good seasons out of Larkin, Sabo, Hatcher, and Duncan. Newcomers Glenn Braggs and Hal Morris were both hitting over .300, while Davis was up to .241 with 10 homers. Armstrong was still the best starter at 10-3. Tom Browning was at 7-5, while Rijo was 5-3.

The relievers continued to stand out. Dibble was 4-2 with 7 saves and a 1.67 ERA. He had fanned 68 in just 43 innings. Myers was 3-2 with 14 saves and a 2.41 ERA. He had 52 Ks in 41 innings. Charlton was 5-1 with two saves and had struck out 50 in 43 frames. All three were devasting, though Dibble was complaining that he didn't want to be a setup man but rather the co-closer with Myers. But a little anger never hurt any team.

Then, just when it seemed as if there would be virtually no race in the National League West, the Reds faltered. They went on a West Coast road trip, won their first game, then lost eight straight. Though they won their final two contests, they returned home

In the eyes of many, Barry Larkin had become baseball's best shortstop in 1990. A fine fielder and improving hitter, Larkin was an important part of the Reds' quest to be baseball's best. *(Courtesy Cincinnati Reds)*

to find their lead over the Giants had slipped from 10 to 5½ games.

"I fully expect this team to regroup, play well, maintain our margin, and win the pennant," said the ever-positive Piniella. "There's no reason in the world we can't win from wire to wire if we do the things we've done in the past. Truthfully, this is the year for this club to win. If not, we might have to break this thing up."

The last thought served as a warning. Piniella was telling his team to take nothing for granted. The manager felt his club had the talent to win. He didn't want his players to feel so secure that they would ease up. While it's unlikely that a team like the Reds would be overhauled just because they lost a lead, it wasn't inconceivable that a number of deals might be made to improve team chemistry.

Almost every good team will run into a slump at some time during the season. During the eight-game losing streak the club had batted just .165 and scored only 14 runs. When they got home, Manager Piniella ordered an extra hour of batting practice every day. Another losing streak could cost them the lead.

The team picked it up a little over the next 26 games, winning 15 and losing 11, bringing their record to 77-55. They still weren't the hot team of early in the year, but they were holding a good lead. The Giants had faltered and were 10½ behind on September 3, while the Dodgers had moved into second and were 6½ back. Only the Oakland A's in the American League, the defending world champs and a ballclub considered the best in baseball, had a better record than the Reds.

Now Cincy was the favorite to win it. With a super

strong bullpen, the team was almost uncatchable once they had the lead after the sixth inning. But they were still waiting for Eric Davis, mired in a long slump, to break loose.

"Some people have a misconception about our team," Piniella said. "It's not the Big Red Machine of the 1970s. We have a nice little team, but it's oriented toward pitching and defense. We win when we get strong pitching, play good defense, and mix in some timely hitting."

Certainly a tried-and-true formula. But as the season drew to a close, there were skeptics about the Reds. The team won the N.L. West with a 91-71 record, finishing five games in front of the Dodgers and six ahead of the Giants. But it was pointed out that Cincy was just 58-59, not even a .500 team, after their torrid 35-12 start. Eastern Division winning Pittsburgh finished with a better record at 95-67, and Oakland led everyone with 103 victories in the A.L. West.

But the Reds won when they had to. Their lead was sliced to 3½ games twice—on August 4 and again on September 20. But each time the ballclub rallied to build it up again.

"Every time the Giants or Dodgers got close, the national media thought we would collapse," said Piniella. "But we proved them wrong. Whenever we needed a win in a big game, we always got it."

The Reds became the first National League team to sit in first place a whole season since the beginning of the 162-game schedule and the start of division play in 1969.

"We started in first place, and we're still in first place," said reliever Rob Dibble, echoing his manager's thoughts. "All year long people have said we can't do it, we can't do it. Well, we did it."

While the Reds were no longer considered overpowering once the year ended, several of their players had put together outstanding seasons. Hal Morris, a former Yankee farmhand, saw more playing time as the year went on and wound up with a .340 batting average in 309 at bats. Duncan hit .306 with 10 homers and 55 RBIs, his best year in the majors. Larkin continued to become a full-fledged superstar with a .301 season, driving in 67 runs and stealing 30 bases. Paul O'Neill had 16 homers and 78 RBIs, while Chris Sabo hit 25 dingers and drove home 71.

And Eric Davis finally shook his long slump to finish with a flourish. He got his average up to .260, hit 24 homers, and led the club with 86 RBIs. It wasn't a typical Davis year, but he showed he was ready for the playoffs. And some final role players like Braggs, Hatcher, Benzinger (who lost his first base job to Morris), Ron Oester, and a good year from catcher Oliver, and the team had the formula for winning.

If there was any weakness, it might have been the starting pitching. But both southpaw Browning (15-9) and right-hander Rijo (14-8) finished strong to compensate for the slump of first half sensation Armstrong, who wound up just 12-9. Danny Jackson spent part of the year injured again, but the veteran lefty finished 6-6 and, more important, was ready for the playoffs. Norm Charlton was also 12-9 and had moved into the rotation during the second half.

Myers and Dibble continued to excel out of the pen. Myers saved 31 with a 2.08 earned run average, fanning 98 in 86.2 innings. Dibble, who didn't close

Slugging outfielder Eric Davis is considered a superstar talent and one of baseball's top all-around players. His biggest problem has been avoiding injuries, many of which have been caused by his all-out effort in the outfield. *(Courtesy Cincinnati Reds)*

as much, was even more spectacular. He finished at 8-3 with 11 saves and a 1.74 ERA. He also fanned 136 hitters in just 98 innings. Either reliever could obviously do the job.

In the playoffs the Reds would be meeting old rival Pittsburgh, featuring the slugging duo of Barry Bonds (who would be the league MVP) and Bobby Bonilla. On the mound the Bucs were led by Doug Drabek, who won 22 games and would win the Cy Young Award. While the Pirates had strong support with the bats (Andy Van Slyke, Sid Bream, and others), their secondary starters were just average and the bullpen couldn't match the Reds'.

The playoff series opened at Riverfront Stadium in Cincinnati. There were 52,911 fans on hand to watch Jose Rijo go up against Bob Walk of the Bucs. It started as if the Reds were going to run away with it. After the Pirates went down in order in the first, Cincy came up and almost KO'd Walk. Morris, Davis, and O'Neill all drove in first-inning runs as the Reds jumped in front, 3–0. But after that the Pirate pitchers toughened, and the Bucs began to chip away at the lead.

They got a run back in the third, and then in the fourth Rijo walked Barry Bonds with two out. For some reason Rijo kept throwing to first. Eight straight times he went to the bag instead of the plate. And when he finally threw a pitch to Sid Bream, he had lost his concentration, and Bream put the ball over the right field wall for a game-tying, two-run homer.

By the seventh Norm Charlton was in the ballgame, and the Bucs scored again, this time on a defensive lapse by the usually reliable Eric Davis. Davis misjudged a drive by Andy Van Slyke, allowing the ball to drop behind him in left for a run-scoring double. That made it 4–3, and it was the Pittsburgh relievers who reversed the roles and made the lead stand up.

Suddenly the Reds were in trouble. Pittsburgh had won the opener in Cincy. If they could also win the second game, the road would be extremely rocky for the Reds. Piniella sent Tom Browning to the hill to face 22-game winner Doug Drabek. Pittsburgh jumped on Browning in the first inning as the leadoff man Gary Redus singled, followed by a base hit by Jay Bell.

"I knew I was in trouble," Browning said later, "but if you worry about a situation like that, you wind up making more mistakes. I just tried to keep my composure."

He did, getting Van Slyke on a fly out, Bonilla on a foul pop, and Bonds via the strikeout route. Browning's clutch pitching gave the team a shot in the arm. They got another break when they built a run against Drabek in the first on a walk and base hits by Herm Winningham and O'Neill.

It stayed that way until the fifth, when the Pirates' Jose Lind touched Browning for a solo homer. But the Reds regained the lead in the bottom of the inning. Once again it was Paul O'Neill doing the damage, driving home Winningham with a clutch double. It was now 2–1. Browning pitched the first six, then the Nasty Boys took over. First Dibble, then Myers came on to close it out and even the playoffs at a game apiece.

Then, beginning in the third game, a pattern began to emerge. The Pirates began getting little or no production from their 3-4-5 hitters, Van Slyke, Bonilla, and Bonds. They were a trio who had 311 RBIs together during the regular season. Now they began leaving men on base in one clutch situation after another.

In Game Three the Reds broke open a 2–2 deadlock with three runs in the top of the fifth, making the score 5–2 against southpaw Zane Smith. Danny Jackson pitched well for 5.1 innings. Then all three Nasty Boys took a turn finishing up. The final was 6–3, and the Reds had the lead. The hitting star was Billy Hatcher, who had three hits, including a two-run homer, his first circuit shot in five weeks. But that's the mark of a great team. Someone steps forward to do what has to be done.

The same pattern prevailed in the fourth game as Rijo and Walk hooked up once again. The Pirates took a 1–0 lead in the first. Cincy made it 2–1 in the fourth, only to have Pittsburgh tie it again in the bottom of the inning. But a pair of Cincy tallies in the seventh and one more in the ninth ensured a 5–3 victory. This time it was Chris Sabo who had the big day, lofting a sacrifice fly and then whacking a two-run homer to provide the margin of victory.

Now it was the Bucs who were hurting. Cincy had a commanding 3–1 lead and sent Tom Browning up against Doug Drabek in an attempt to wrap it up. But Drabek and the Bucs were just a little better, winning 3–2 and sending the playoffs back to Cincinnati for a sixth game. Danny Jackson would be opposed by surprise starter Ted Power.

Cincy got a run in the first as Davis picked up the RBI. By the third, righty Power was out, and lefty Zane Smith was in. The quick change might have been an attempt by the Pirates' Jim Leyland to neutralize the Reds lineup and force Manager Piniella into some early moves. But it stayed 1–0 until the fifth when Pittsburgh pushed across the tying run. Then came the Cincinnati seventh.

Ron Oester opened the frame with a single. With one out, a base hit by Hatcher sent Oester to third. Now switch-hitter Luis Quinones came up to pinch-hit for O'Neill. It was a daring gamble by Piniella because O'Neill had been a hot hitter. But the manager felt the lefty slants of Zane Smith could handcuff O'Neill. Sure enough, Quinones singled home Oester with what proved to be the winning run. Charlton and Myers pitched the last three innings, and the Reds were National League champions.

They had done it with some great defense and clutch pitching, two of the elements Piniella said his team needed in order to win.

"I kept waiting for their outfielders to make a throwing error," said the Bucs' Van Slyke. "But they're almost robotic out there."

And closer Randy Myers said, "I was surprised that we were able to keep their big hitters off-balance. They are a *great* hitting team."

But the Reds had done it, silencing many critics at the same time. But now they had to get ready for the supreme test. In the World Series they would be going up against defending champion Oakland. The powerful A's had eliminated the Boston Red Sox in four straight games. The A's already had the reputation as being a Super Team, but to solidify it really, they wanted a second straight World Series triumph. The ballclub had been upset by the Dodgers in 1988 but came back to sweep the Giants a year ago. Now they were prepared to take on the Reds.

The A's, of course, had power plus with Jose Canseco, Mark McGwire, Dave and Rickey Henderson, and Harold Baines. They had speed with stolen base king Rickey Henderson leading the way, and great pitching, with starters like Dave Stewart, Bob Welch, and Mike Moore. Plus, they had the man considered to be the best closer in the game—Dennis Eckersley. They were overwhelming favorites.

But the applecart started to be upset in the opening game, in fact, in the first inning. It was Rijo against Stewart at Riverfront when the Reds came up in the bottom of the first. With one out Billy Hatcher singled, and two batters later Eric Davis put Stewart's first pitch over the wall for a two-run homer.

Cincy then touched up Stewart for another pair in the third, giving them a 4–0 lead. Then came a key play. In the fifth the A's loaded the bases with two out and had slugger Mark McGwire up. They could have tied it with one swing of the bat. But Rijo reached back for something extra and fanned him.

"I made a mistake," Rijo admitted later. "I threw a slider with poor location and let him swing under the ball. I was lucky."

But it was more than luck as Rijo threw seven innings of seven-hit shutout ball. Dibble and Myers finished up with an inning apiece of relief, and the Reds had a 7–0 victory. Then came the second game, and when this one ended, the A's should have seen the handwriting on the wall.

It was the kind of game the A's didn't lose very often. They scored a run in the first off Danny Jackson, but then up came the Reds. Four pitches later they had a 2–1 lead. Barry Larkin started it off with a double, a ball that many thought right fielder Jose

Canseco should have caught. But Canseco was suffering with a painful back, and it slowed him up in the field and at the plate. Two pitches later Hatcher blasted a home run, and the Reds were back in front.

But the A's weren't about to lie down. They came back to knock Jackson out in the third when they scored three times. With 27-game winner Bob Welch on the mound, a 4–2 lead seemed pretty safe. But the Reds chipped away for a run in the fourth. It was 4–3 and stayed that way until the last of the eighth. Welch was still on the hill, and many wondered why Manager LaRussa didn't bring in Eckersley right then and there. After all, he was the best closer in baseball.

The move backfired immediately. Hatcher slammed a triple, and LaRussa still waited two more hitters before making a move. Then he called on Rick Honeycutt, and the Reds tied the game on an infield out. When Eckersley finally got the call, it was the bottom of the 10th, the score still tied. The usually unhittable reliever promptly gave up singles to pinch hitter Billy Bates, Chris Sabo, and Joe Oliver. Bates scored on Oliver's hit, and the Reds had won it, 5–4.

"I went up there. I didn't want to lose it. I wanted the big hit," said catcher Oliver. It was another example of all the Cincinnati players coming through. In fact, the A's still hadn't gotten Billy Hatcher out. After two games the centerfielder had seven hits in seven trips with a couple of walks. Even though the Series was moving to Oakland, the A's still had a long way back.

It got longer after Game Three. Tom Browning started against Mike Moore, and all the scoring came in the first three innings. Fortunately for the Reds, eight of those runs came in their column. Though neither team scored in the first, the Reds gave a hint of things to come. They had three singles in the opening frame but were turned back. In the second Chris Sabo slammed a solo home run, and Cincy was back in front once more.

Then in the bottom of the inning the A's finally had something to cheer about. Designated hitter Harold Baines slammed a Browning offering over the right field wall for a two-run homer that gave the A's the lead. The crowd of 48,269 roared in approval. Now maybe their heroes would begin to unpack the lumber.

Unfortunately, it was the Reds who unpacked. In the third inning Cincinnati unloaded to score seven runs, six of them officially unearned after a Mark McGwire error. They KO'd Moore and greeted reliever Scott Sanderson with three straight hits. Sabo, who homered an inning earlier, came back to blast a two-run shot in the third to highlight the outburst. Though the A's managed a single tally in the bottom of the frame, it was still an 8–3 game. Cincinnati had 11 hits after just three innings, and 14 of the 23 Reds who came to the plate had reached base. It was complete devastation.

From there the pitching took over. Browning went six-plus, then Dibble and Myers finished up, yielding just one hit over the final three. The A's relievers also held the Reds, but it was too late. The final was 8–3, the Cincinnati had themselves a third straight win.

"Our young guys had to play pressure ball all year," said Cincy pitching coach Stan Williams. "We didn't make a habit of blowing out anybody. In fact,

Third sacker Chris Sabo was the National League Rookie of the Year in 1988. Two years later he was a maturing hitter who was instrumental in helping the Reds to a World Series sweep of the heavily favored Oakland A's. *(Courtesy Cincinnati Reds)*

we spent most of the season 'eeking' people out. I can't remember a lot of games when we scored eight runs like we did today.''

It was Stewart and Rijo again in Game Four. In this one Manager LaRussa benched Jose Canseco because of his ailing back, and in the eyes of many that was tantamount to surrender. The A's, of course, didn't see it that way. They quickly scored a run in the first on hits by Willie McGee and Carney Lansford. While no one could know it at the time, those would be the only two hits the A's would get all game.

Rijo then settled into an incredible groove, pitching hitless ball for 7⅔ innings and retiring the last 20 hitters he faced. But until the top of the eighth inning, he still trailed by a 1–0 score, as Stewart regained the form that made him one of the great postseason pitchers in modern times. As Rijo came off the field after retiring the A's in the seventh, he barked at his teammates, telling them he was tired of watching them blow opportunities and to get out there and score a couple of runs.

Know what? They did. And they did it without Eric Davis and Billy Hatcher, both of whom had to leave the game with injuries. They did it because Herm Winningham, who went in for Hatcher, was able to beat out a surprise bunt. They did it because pitcher Stewart made a throwing error on a sacrifice bunt by Paul O'Neill that allowed the Reds to load the bases with none out. They did it because the A's failed to turn a double play on a grounder by Glenn Braggs that got one run home. And they did it when Hal Morris hit another grounder that allowed the second run to cross the plate.

Rijo retired the A's in the eighth, then got one out in the ninth before giving way to Myers. The veteran lefty closed out the A's without any damage, and the Reds had won the game, 2–1, and the World Series with an improbable four-game sweep. The Reds had beaten the supposedly best team in baseball and had made it look easy. Manager Piniella was overjoyed.

"From day one we worked on developing a winning attitude here," he said. "We worked on the chemistry aspect. And we worked on fundamentals. I told the players, 'If you do things in the way they should be done, you'll win games.' "

Win, they did. They got great pitching, solid defense, and timely hitting. Billy Hatcher, for instance, had 9 hits in 12 at bats for a series record .750 average for four games. Larkin, Sabo, and Davis also hit well, and the other guys came through when it counted. The Reds pitchers also held the Bash Brothers Canseco and McGwire, to four total hits. After getting three hits in the opener, Rickey Henderson had just two more over the next three games.

The A's had to be disappointed in the loss, and it was Carney Lansford who said what a lot of people were thinking.

"I felt that in order for us to be classified as a special team, we had to win the Series. But if you drop two [World Series] in three years, you can't be considered a great team yet."

So what about the Reds? They were certainly super early in the year, then coasted to the divisional title. In the playoffs and Series they became a Super Team once again, showing all the elements needed to win. They were surely a Super Team when they had to be. Whether they can do that over a long haul remains to be seen. One person, however, who was not surprised by the Reds' victory was Joe Morgan, who had played for the Big Red Machine in the late 1970s and was a recent inductee into the Hall of Fame.

"The Reds won because their pitching matched up perfectly against the A's and because they have better athletes," said Morgan. "They also played together as a team. There's no doubt in my mind that the best team won."

ABOUT THE AUTHOR

BILL GUTMAN has been an avid sports fan ever since he can remember. A freelance writer for twenty years, he has done profiles and bios of many of today's sports heroes. Mr. Gutman has written about all of the major sports and some lesser ones as well. In addition to profiles and bios, he has also written sports instructional books and sports fiction. He is the author of Archway's *Sports Illustrated* series; *Bo Jackson: A Biography; Pro Sports Champions;* and *Michael Jordan: A Biography,* available from Archway Paperbacks. Currently, he lives in Poughquag, New York, with his wife, two stepchildren, and a variety of pets.